'I can't believe no man has wanted you.'

'I've never met one *I* wanted.' Until I saw *you* walking across the lobby, Marly thought. 'I believe marriage is for life, Mr Hamilton, and I will have to be absolutely certain about a man before I commit myself to him.'

'When you're my age you'll know nothing is certain in life.'

Except for one thing, Marly knew: her determination to cut this man down to size.

D0530829

Next month sees a great new look for our Romances—and we can guarantee you'll enjoy our stories just as much. Passionate, sensual, warm and tender—at heart, Mills & Boon Romances are as satisfying as ever.

THE EDITOR

Dear Reader

Over the past year, along with our usual wide variety of exciting romances, you will, we hope, have been enjoying a romantic journey around Europe with our Euromance series. From this month, you'll be able to have double the fun and double the passion, as there will now be two Euromance books each month—one set in one of your favourite European countries, and one on a fascinating European island. Remember to pack your passport!

The Editor

Roberta Leigh is a workaholic, but loves every minute of it! How else could she have produced 150 romances, been columnist on a national newspaper, written 27 children's books and created and produced 247 films for children? But romantic fiction has a special place in her life, and she was one of the first writers to introduce strong, career-minded heroines who wouldn't be bossed around by the hero! She lives in London, loves children, dogs and cats and, since the death of her husband, finds her romance in the books she loves writing.

Recent titles by the same author:

BACHELOR AT HEART
TWO-TIMING MAN

GIVE A MAN
A BAD NAME

BY

ROBERTA LEIGH

MILLS & BOON LIMITED
ETON HOUSE,   18-24 PARADISE ROAD
RICHMOND,   SURREY   TW9 1SR

All the characters in this book have no existence outside the imagination of the Author, and have no relation whatsoever to anyone bearing the same name or names. They are not even distantly inspired by any individual known or unknown to the Author, and all the incidents are pure invention.

All Rights Reserved. The text of this publication or any part thereof may not be reproduced or transmitted in any form or by any means, electronic or mechanical, including photocopying, recording, storage in an information retrieval system, or otherwise, without the written permission of the publisher.

This book is sold subject to the condition that it shall not, by way of trade or otherwise, be lent, resold, hired out or otherwise circulated without the prior consent of the publisher in any form of binding or cover other than that in which it is published and without a similar condition including this condition being imposed on the subsequent purchaser.

*First published in Great Britain 1993
by Mills & Boon Limited*

© Roberta Leigh 1993

*Australian copyright 1993
Philippine copyright 1993
This edition 1993*

ISBN 0 263 78217 4

*Set in Times Roman 10 on 11¼ pt.
01-9309-53783 C*

Made and printed in Great Britain

CHAPTER ONE

WHEN Marly Bradshaw saw Alex Hamilton for the first time, she knew he was the man of her dreams.

It was an unusually romantic thought for a young woman who had always considered herself practical and intelligent; more interested in her career than cooking, in climbing the corporate ladder than catering to a husband's whims.

And yet . . .

'He affected me that way too,' her closest friend Nan commented. 'Even now my heart thumps when I see him.'

'He probably has a squeaky voice and a wife and four kids!' Marly grinned.

Nan shook her head so vigorously that her thick black hair, permed into a riot of curls, bounced around her head. 'He has the sexiest deep brown voice and he's single.'

Further conversation was cut short by Nan being called to Reception, and Marly, returning to her office, thought for the umpteenth time what a stroke of luck it was that Steve Rivers, her boss at 3S Software in London, had asked her if she would consider going to Thailand to set up a computer program for the Riverside Hamilton, the newest luxury hotel of the Hamilton chain.

'Consider it?' she had exclaimed. 'Why, I'd jump at it! My great-grandmother was Thai, and it's my favourite country in all the world.'

'Mine too,' Steve had agreed. 'How did your great-grandpa meet his wife? Thailand wasn't a tourist spot in those days.'

'He was a diplomat, and so was her father. They met at an embassy party and it was love at first sight.'

A month later had found Marly in Bangkok, staying with Nan Damrong and her parents. The two girls had met at boarding-school, and since then Marly had visited Thailand every other year, so that the prospect of seeing Nan for a couple of months had made the job doubly attractive.

Arriving at the Riverside for her first day of work, she had been disconcerted to discover that Alex Hamilton, heir to the business and temporary manager of its newest hotel, had been called to a board meeting in New York, leaving her to kick her heels till he returned and told her exactly how he wanted her to prepare the software.

Chafing at the delay, she had none the less used it to learn as much about the running of the hotel as possible, knowing it would help her devise the most efficient program. She had also renewed her acquaintance with Bangkok, for in the two years since she had been here it had changed considerably, with the addition of two more luxury hotels, another huge shopping complex, and high-rise office blocks mushrooming everywhere.

She had been delighted to find her knowledge of Thai—originally learned from Nan and then perfected by tapes and discs—was as good as ever, thanks to an aptitude for foreign languages. Indeed, one afternoon wandering the crowded streets, she had haggled over the price of a blouse and been mistaken for a Thai! As she was petite and fine-boned, with silky black hair inherited from her great-grandmother, and almond-shaped brown eyes inherited from a Cornish grandfather, this wasn't surprising. And even after she had produced her passport to prove it, the local man had not been entirely convinced.

She was still amused by the incident when, returning to the Riverside, she had her first glimpse of Alex Hamilton. Not that she had known who he was. She had been standing by the magazine stall to one side of the huge marble foyer, when an unusual bustle at the vast plate-glass entrance doors made her turn to see what it was about. Yet another VIP, she had assumed, and expecting one to saunter in, had instead seen a very tall man with hair thick and tawny as a lion's mane stride smartly across the floor, accompanied by scurrying minions.

Curious to know who he was, she had moved forward, not realising she was in his path until he stopped and frowned. Not even the drawing together of strongly marked eyebrows could mar the handsome face, for which the word 'chiselled' was singularly apt. High cheekbones swept down to a firm jaw, redeemed from squareness by a cleft chin, and deep-set eyes—the grey of woodland smoke—raked her from head to toe.

If he had run his hands over her body her reaction could not have been more startled. It was as if she had been given a shot of adrenalin. Her pulses raced, her breathing quickened, and the world seemed a brighter, more exciting place.

I'm mad, she thought, quite mad! But she knew she wasn't; she was simply aware that for the first time in her life her innermost core had been touched. Colour came and went in her cheeks and she mumbled an apology and stepped back, glad of the huge dark glasses half covering her face.

Acknowledging her movement with a faint smile, which drew her attention to his mobile, well shaped mouth, he strode past her, and as he disappeared into a lift, still accompanied by members of the hotel staff, she asked a passing bellboy who he was.

'Mr Hamilton,' came the reply.

Stunned, she had stared at the lift doors. So that was the man who was to be her boss for the next two months! The prospect was as full of spice as gingerbread, and she had raced up the wide, carpeted stairs to the mezzanine floor that led to the offices, intent on sharing her experience with Nan.

'He's a real dreamboat, isn't he?' her friend had agreed. 'But not an easy man to know. He plays his cards close to his chest.'

'Does he have a girlfriend?'

'In the plural. They line up for him and fall at his feet like ninepins. But he's soon off with the old and on with the new.'

Marly was mulling this over as she slid into the passenger seat of Nan's car to go home, though she did not mull for long, for she was soon holding on to her seat for dear life. Nan, in common with the majority of Thais, drove fast: weaving in and out of traffic, dodging oncoming cars, taxis and tuk-tuks—three-wheeled scooter taxis—and skimming so close to them that she practically scraped their paintwork!

But when a motorcyclist cut in front of them for no reason other than to mount a pavement and park his bike there, Marly had had enough and shut her eyes tight. But she opened them again immediately, deciding it was easier to cope with seen fear. Heart in mouth, she watched Nan shoot along the inside lane, overtake a single-decker bus with people clinging to the doors like limpets, and swing sharply left into the quiet side-street where she lived.

'I'll never get used to the way you drive,' Marly gasped, emerging from the car outside her friend's home.

Large, beautiful, and built of golden teak, it was in the Thai gabled roof tradition, and could have been mistaken for two houses instead of one, had it not been for the balcony joining them together on the upper floor. It was also quite a rarity among Bangkok's newer single-storeyed houses with their corrugated-iron roofs, though recently the traditional had started coming back into favour, albeit at exorbitant prices.

Leaving their shoes by the front door before stepping over the threshold—as was the custom—they walked into the living-room and, with palms together and heads bowed, *waied* Nan's mother in the time-honoured greeting towards Thai elders and superiors.

Since first visiting her friend, Marly had been touched by such customs, for they indicated a respect and caring for each other that was endemic to Thai culture.

'Your father is bringing Kevin Rossiter back with him from the hospital,' Nan's mother told them. In a pastel-blue cheong-sam, the traditional dress still favoured by many Thai women, she was smaller than her daughter, with silky, grey-streaked hair drawn into a coil at the nape of her neck. 'Kevin is a brilliant young doctor and has been working with the professor for the past month,' she explained to Marly.

'Is he staying for dinner?' Nan questioned.

'He'll be very welcome if he does,' her mother replied, surveying the table the maid had set with more places than the size of her family. Thai hospitality was legendary, their homes and food being shared with anyone who cared to accept it.

Twenty minutes later Marly and her friend, showered and changed into softly shaded dresses, returned to the living-room where Nan's father was talking to a sandy-haired young man.

'Kevin's from New Zealand and is studying tropical medicine in my department,' Professor Damrong, a stockily built man a little taller than his wife, informed Marly.

Smiling at the visitor, Marly saw only Alex Hamilton's face staring down at her—Alex Hamilton of the smoky grey eyes, chiselled features and supercilious smile, the man whose path she had blocked earlier that day.

'Marly and my daughter were at school together in England,' the professor went on. 'She's here to prepare a computer program for the Riverside Hamilton.'

'Sounds a big job,' Kevin commented, warm hazel eyes intent on her. 'Why don't you and Nan have dinner with me and put me in the picture? I'm a computer nut.'

'You two go,' Nan said promptly. 'I'm behind with my lines and have three days left to learn them.'

'Lines?' Kevin quizzed.

'For the cabaret the staff at the hotel are putting on for Christmas.'

'Looks as if it's just the two of us,' Kevin said to Marly, and she tried to look pleased at the prospect.

Her brief encounter with Alex Hamilton had put her on an emotional high, and she was in no mood to make conversation with an earnest young doctor, worthy though he might be. But once seated opposite him in the Italian restaurant of the Royal Orchid Hotel, she was glad she had accepted his invitation. After all, it was stupid to behave like a lovesick schoolgirl over a man who did not know she existed!

'It's a stroke of luck meeting you,' Kevin commented after they had given their order. 'I hope you're going to be here for several months?'

'I'm not sure. It depends how long it takes me to devise the software that the hotel wants.'

'Is it just for the hotel here?'

'No. For the whole group.'

'Obviously a very high-powered woman.' Kevin looked flatteringly impressed. 'Is there a boyfriend in the background?'

Marly shook her head. 'Not even in the foreground! I've been too busy with my career. What about you?'

'Fancy-free and still looking! Like you, I've been too busy establishing myself. Still, the worst is behind me and the future is for living,' he said, signalling the waiter to pour their wine.

Sipping it, Marly studied him through her lashes. He was a nice-looking man if you fancied them fair, hazel-eyed and whipcord-thin. Except that she preferred them tawny-haired, smoky-eyed and powerfully built.

'Tell me about your job,' Kevin cut across her musing. 'Or don't you like talking shop?'

'I love it,' she grinned. 'But right now there's nothing much to tell. My boss was away until today, and I haven't yet found out what my brief is.'

'When did you arrive?'

'A week ago, and I've been champing at the bit till now. Though to be honest I love wandering around Bangkok.'

'Maybe we can wander together,' he suggested. 'How are you fixed for tomorrow? I'm always free on a Sunday.'

'I'm not. At least not this Sunday,' Marly lied, reluctant to give him any encouragement. 'Now that Mr Hamilton's back I'd better stay in the Riverside.'

'Fair enough. But if you think I'm letting you off the hook...'

She smiled at his persistence and tactfully changed the subject. 'How long are you here for?'

'Six months. Before that I was doing a course in the States.'

'What do you think of the standard of medicine there?'

Marly had hit on one of his hobby-horses, and for the remainder of the evening she managed to keep the conversation away from herself.

'I'll call you in a couple of days,' Kevin said when he delivered her home.

'Fine. By then I should know what free time I'll have.'

As she let herself into the house, she forgot him completely. Strange that one uncaring man could bowl you over in a second, and another—striving for hours to make a good impression—could leave no impression whatever.

'Enjoy yourself?' Nan asked, bouncing into Marly's room as she climbed into bed.

'It was pleasant enough.'

'Poor Kevin! That sounds like the kiss of death!'

'He's a nice guy but——'

'He doesn't set you on fire.'

'That's the story of my life!' Marly yawned and stretched her arms above her head. 'Are you rehearsing tomorrow?'

'Until late afternoon. And you?'

'I'm going to take it easy.'

'You've done nothing else for a week!'

'Blame Mr Hamilton,' Marly said sleepily. 'See you at breakfast.'

'I'll be gone before you get up,' Nan answered, and switching off the centre light, left the room.

Emerging from the shower next morning, Marly heard a light tap at her door, and Ying, the youngest of the family's four servants, told her she was wanted on the telephone. It was probably Kevin. He had not believed her excuse and had decided to try his luck again. Wrapping a towel round her, she hurried down to the living-room and picked up the receiver.

The voice at the other end was so unexpected, she nearly dropped it.

'Andrea! How marvellous to hear from you. You sound so close.'

'I am. I'm at Bangkok airport. The plane made an emergency landing here due to engine trouble.'

'Have you finished your teaching job in Singapore?'

'Yes. Well, to be honest, I resigned. I had to get away.'

'What went wrong?'

'I can't talk on the phone. Is there any chance of you coming to the airport to see me?'

'Of course,' Marly said instantly. 'How long do you have?'

'A couple of hours. Get here soon, will you? I'll wait for you in the main cafeteria.'

Marly hurried to her room to dress. She, Nan and Andrea had been inseparable at school, and had remained in touch through lengthy letters and the occasional telephone call. It was almost six months since she and Andrea had met, and it would be wonderful to see her again, though her tone of voice did not augur a happy meeting. Still, that was when one needed one's friends.

Nan's driving was as nothing to the forty-five-minute taxi ride Marly had to endure along the Expressway to Don Muang Airport, and as she entered the air-conditioned concourse she felt more in need of a stiff brandy than mid-morning coffee!

Her first sight of Andrea gave her a shock, for the radiant blonde she had last seen was now a picture of abject misery: hair without lustre, eyes puffy with unshed tears, and a once curvaceous figure angular.

'Darling!' Marly exclaimed, clasping her close. 'What's happened to you?'

Tears spilling over, Andrea told her.

It was a man, of course. The most fabulous man in Singapore—an Adonis, naturally!—with wit, charm, and money in abundance. A whirlwind courtship had been followed by a proposal of marriage, after which she had moved in with him. Then six weeks ago he had announced that he had changed his mind about marriage, packed his bags and departed for Italy.

'Try a Dutchman next time,' Marly advised, trying to lighten her friend's mood. 'Italians are known for their roving eye.'

'He's English,' Andrea corrected. 'He was going to Italy to take charge of a hotel his family owns there, and I'm pretty certain he's got another woman in Rome.'

'Odd that he's in the hotel business,' Marly put in ironically. 'So is my temporary boss, and he's also a walking Adonis.'

'Steer clear of him, then,' Andrea muttered. 'At least ugly men are grateful if you fancy them! Alex simply took it for granted. Not surprising, considering the way the girls chased him.'

'Alex?' Marly echoed, her pulse jumping erratically. 'What's his last name?'

'Hamilton.'

Unbelievable! It *was* her boss. So much for meeting the man of her dreams. After the story she had just heard, he could best be described as every girl's nightmare.

Marly wondered whether to tell her friend that her ex-fiancé had lied about going to Rome, and was actually in charge of the family hotel in Bangkok where, far from being with one woman, he would happily be taking his pick of a line-up! But Andrea was unhappy enough as it was, and it would serve little purpose to inform her that the man she still loved wasn't merely a philanderer but a liar into the bargain!

'He sounds a real swine,' she said instead. 'Forget him.'

'I wish I could,' Andrea answered miserably. 'But I still love him. Perhaps I shouldn't have moved in with him. I feel as if I've let myself down.'

'That's crazy talk, Andrea. It's Alex who's let you down, not yourself.'

Yet though Marly said this she found it easy to empathise with her friend, who was echoing Nan's feelings as well as hers. At sixteen they had all made the same vow, and maturity had not changed their minds. Sex without love was something they abhorred, and no matter how much their other friends teased them for their old-fashioned views, they had held firm to them.

'Perhaps if I hadn't gone to bed with him, he might have married me,' Andrea said into the silence.

'You can't believe a marriage licence would tie down a man of his type?'

'I suppose not.' Tears fell fast and Andrea fumbled for her handkerchief. 'He was so wonderful, Marly. Unbelievably handsome and charming.'

'Unbelievable being the operative word,' Marly retorted. 'Forget him. He's not worth a moment's thought. You're young and beautiful, and you'll soon be rhapsodising over someone more worthwhile.'

Having almost convinced Andrea of this by the time her plane was ready to continue its flight, Marly returned to the city a little easier in her mind. What a nasty trick of fate that Alex Hamilton should turn out to be the biggest pig this side of Eden! Who cared if he was Adonis in looks and charismatic in character? Much better if he had been honest and loyal. But why was she getting so hot under the collar over a man she had merely glimpsed in the entrance lobby of a hotel? It was quite on the cards that if she waited by the magazine stall again she would see a dozen equally handsome and magnetic men!

'Enjoy your day?' Nan enquired, coming into Marly's bedroom later that afternoon, where she sat brushing up her Thai from a television film.

'Not especially. I saw Andrea.'

'She's *here*?'

'Not any longer.' Briefly Marly recounted Andrea's story, and had the dubious pleasure of seeing Nan become as furious as herself.

'I know Mr Hamilton plays the field, but I never imagined he'd ask a girl to marry him and then walk out on her. Are you sure she wasn't exaggerating?'

'Oh, come on, Nan, you know Andrea better than that. She may look like a dumb blonde, but she certainly isn't one. Believe me, I've never seen her so devastated.'

'I wish you'd persuaded her to stay with us for a week or so.'

'I was going to suggest it, but I was worried she might bump into him here. I didn't tell her he hadn't gone to Rome.'

'I'd forgotten that.' Nan sank cross-legged to the floor. 'A good thing you discovered the sort of man he is. From the way you reacted when you saw him, you might have become the next discard!'

Marly was honest enough not to deny it.

'Think you can take another shock?' Nan ventured.

'Depends.'

'We need someone to replace Siri, the other Thai girl in the cabaret. She's gone down with bronchitis.'

'So why tell *me*?' Marly asked.

'Because the part calls for a Thai, and you can pass for one.'

'But I've never acted in my life!'

'All females know how to act!'

'Maybe, but not on stage.'

'What's the difference? Be a sport, Marly. Siri was only in one sketch, and with your photographic memory you'll waltz through it.'

Marly sighed, swayed by Nan's downcast expression. 'Very well, but don't blame me if I flop.'

'You won't. You'll be wonderful!'

'What if Mr Hamilton won't give me time off to rehearse? Now he's back he may expect me to get cracking on the software.'

'Find out and let me know.'

Next morning Marly hung around restlessly in her office waiting to be summoned to meet Alex Hamilton, and when lunchtime came and went without a call, she bearded his English secretary, Miss Granger.

'Sorry I didn't contact you before now,' the girl apologised. 'I meant to, but it's been hectic here. Mr Hamilton asked me to apologise on his behalf, and say he won't be able to see you for several days. He was away longer than he anticipated and has a mass of work to catch up on.'

Far from being upset by this, Marly was relieved. She was still seething over his treatment of Andrea, and might have found it difficult to hide her feelings. But this respite would not only give her a chance to learn her lines and rehearse for the show, but also enable her to get used to the idea of working for a man she thoroughly despised.

CHAPTER TWO

'YOU'RE not totally deaf, I presume?'

The raised male voice coming from the next-door office to Marly's made her look up from her terminal in surprise, and unashamedly she eavesdropped. From his tone, the man was in a rousing temper.

'Or perhaps you're on a higher plane and haven't heard anything I've told you?' he went on.

'I did exactly what you asked me to do, Mr Hamilton,' a woman protested, and Marly instantly recognised it as Alex Hamilton's secretary.

'In your own stupid way, Miss Granger!'

'Look, Mr Hamilton——'

'No, *you* look! If you can't follow simple instructions, maybe you should return to the typing pool.'

'Maybe I will!'

There followed a burst of tears and a sharp male curse, and Marly, on the verge of going to comfort the girl as she heard a door slam, stopped at the sound of Alex Hamilton's voice. It was his secretary who had stormed out, not him.

'Personnel!' she heard him bark. 'Assign Miss Granger to someone more long-suffering than me, and send me a replacement. What? No, keep her on the same salary she was receiving.'

To pay off his conscience, no doubt, Marly seethed, casting daggers at the wall dividing her from this most horrible of men. If she were self-employed and did not have a responsibility to her company, she would walk in and tell him what she thought of him! If he was ex-

18

pecting *her* to bow and scrape to him, he had another think coming!

She was still seething when she arrived for rehearsals in the hotel ballroom late that afternoon, though she soon calmed down as Richard, the young director of the cabaret, who normally worked in Accounts, put her through her paces. Her part couldn't have been easier, given her retentive memory, for all she had to do was to learn six pages of dialogue, and spend the rest of her time looking sweet and gentle and quietly amused by the embarrassing antics of the Western visitors to her stage parents' home.

'You were terrific!' Richard exclaimed as rehearsals ended for the day. 'For a gag, we won't put your surname in the programme and will just name you as "Marly". Then the audience will automatically assume you're Thai.'

'Which they'd never do if you printed "Amalia Bradshaw",' she chuckled, and was glad she had let Nan persuade her to participate in the show. It would at least keep her occupied while she was waiting for Alex Hamilton to clear his desk and spare her his time.

By the evening of the performance she was proficient in every word and mannerism of her part, and took equal pains with her appearance, emphasising the exotic slant of her eyes by skilful use of black eyeliner, and parting her hair in the centre so that it fell in a black satin curtain down either side of her face. Wow! She looked just like her great-grandmother.

The sketch she was in was the most successful one of the show, and as it came to an end many people in the audience called out to her in Thai as she accepted a vociferous ovation.

However, some of her pleasure ebbed when she saw Alex Hamilton sitting in the front row, vigorously applauding her. Their eyes met and he half inclined his head and raked her from head to toe as he continued clapping, the gesture truly revealing the sort of man he was! Poor Andrea! If this two-timing Lothario thought he had found another heart to break, he could go jump in a lake—and drown there while he was about it!

With a sigh of relief she watched the audience disperse for the Christmas party that was being held in an adjacent conference-room, and suddenly decided not to attend.

'Where are you going?' Nan stopped her halfway down the corridor, as Marly made for the powder-room to change out of her stage clothes.

'Home,' she replied. 'I'm tired.'

'And I'm Mickey Mouse! For heaven's sake, this is your friend you're trying to kid. What's up? You were the star of the show and everyone will want to meet you.'

'That's what worries me. Did you see the way Alex Hamilton eyed me? As if I were a nut cutlet and he was a starving vegetarian!'

'So what? You'll have to meet him soon anyway. That's why you're here, remember?'

'You have a nasty habit of being right,' Marly sighed. 'I suppose I'd better go change and join you.'

'You look marvellous as you are!'

'But——'

'Come on, Marly, if we hang around any longer, the party will be over.'

Somewhat apprehensively, Marly followed her friend into the green and gold reception-room where the theatre party was being held. Not only were all the clerical and senior staff there, but their families too, and she was soon surrounded by an admiring throng, compliments falling thick around her.

'You're a natural actress...'

'I've never laughed so much...'

'You should be on the stage.'

'You were marvellous...'

'You're also very beautiful,' added a deep, resonant voice, and she looked up, startled, the smile on her lips freezing as she saw Alex Hamilton staring intently down at her.

Close to, he was even more devastating than when she had espied him in the lobby; his tawny, lion's mane hair was flecked with gold where the sun had touched it, and his skin was the colour of pale honey, making his smoke-grey eyes even more remarkable.

'I'm Alex Hamilton,' he introduced himself. 'I see from the programme that you are Marly.'

'Yes,' she managed to say, her mouth so dry she could barely twist her tongue around the word.

'It's a lovely name for a lovely young woman. And you played your part very amusingly; but I suppose it came naturally.'

'Naturally?'

'I assume you've met many Westerners who are as ignorant of your customs as the two actors were in your sketch.'

Heavens, she thought, he *also* thinks I'm Thai! Unable to stop herself, she smiled, and he smiled back. It riveted her eyes to his lips, which were beautifully shaped, the top one well curved, the lower one fuller and sensuous. How many other lips had they kissed? she wondered. How many lies had they told? How many women had he deceived, as he had Andrea?

Drawing herself up to her full height of five feet two inches, she was on the point of telling him exactly who she was, when he spoke again.

'I think it's important to understand the customs of the country one is living in, but sometimes it's not easy to follow them.'

'Are you thinking of anything in particular, Mr Hamilton?'

'Very much so. Normally I'd have no hesitation in asking you to have dinner with me tonight, but since I don't know whether your parents are strict on protocol, I can only suggest that you allow me to take you home and ask them if I may see you again.'

Open-mouthed, she stared at him, and he instantly misinterpreted it.

'I'm sorry if I'm coming on too strong, but you're the loveliest girl I've seen and I'm not letting you walk out of my life.'

Beyond his shoulder she glimpsed Nan mouthing words she could not understand, and she seized this as a means of escape.

'Excuse me a moment, please. I have to give my friend a telephone number.'

'I'll only excuse you if you promise to come straight back,' he said, and turned to watch her as she hurried across to Nan.

'What were you trying to tell me?' Marly asked as she reached her side.

'I wanted to know if you needed rescuing.'

'Every woman under the age of fifty needs rescuing from that man! Talk about charm.' Marly lowered her voice, laughter trembling in it. 'Believe it or not, he thinks I'm Thai. He wants me to have dinner with him but isn't sure whether he has to ask my parents' permission!'

Nan stifled a giggle. 'That must be a first time for him, then.'

Marly nodded, then narrowed her eyes as a thought struck her. A man who had treated Andrea the way Alex Hamilton had clearly had little respect for women. Yet how deferentially he was behaving towards the unliberated girl he thought *her* to be. And not just deferential, but anxious to know her better. Was that because he believed her to be different from the girls he usually favoured? If so, he had just given her a golden opportunity to teach him a well deserved lesson.

Instead of enlightening him, she would continue with her act until he had fallen for her hook, line and sinker. Only then would she disclose her identity, and he would discover that a woman had finally given him his come-uppance, instead of the other way around!

'What scheme are you cooking up?' Nan enquired, recognising from old the mischievousness on Marly's face.

Slanting a glance in Alex Hamilton's direction, and seeing him still watching her, she hurriedly answered her friend's question.

'You'll never be able to keep it up,' Nan gasped.

'Yes, I will. I can't go into it now, there's no time, but we'll talk it over later.'

Leaving Nan still protesting, she glided back to the man waiting for her and gave him a respectful *wai*. 'Thank you for being so patient.'

'You're worth waiting for,' he responded, smoky eyes serious.

For answer, she lowered her head.

'You work here obviously,' he went on, 'or you wouldn't have been in the show, but I don't remember seeing you around.'

'Why should you? You employ so many people.'

'I wouldn't miss *you*.'

'I only started a few days ago.'

'That explains it, then. What do you do?'

'I—I'm a——'

'Never mind,' he cut in, eyes ranging over her butterfly-wing cheong-sam and back to her face. 'You look pale. If you're tired, I'll drive you home.'

'I'm not tired,' she replied softly. 'If your dinner invitation is still open, I will be honoured to accept. You are an important man, and I know my parents would not object.'

'That's marvellous.' Alex Hamilton could not quite hide his elation. 'There are a few people I should say hello to first, then we'll go.'

'As you wish,' she murmured.

'Give me fifteen minutes.'

As he moved off, Nan rushed to her side. 'You were fantastic! Carry on as you are, and you'll have him eating out of your hand.'

'If he doesn't bite it off first!'

'Are you kidding? From the way he was ogling you, it won't take you long to bring him to his knees. It's my bet he'll proposition you before the year's out.'

'That's still ten days away,' Marly hissed, watching the tall, athletic figure circulate among the hotel guests and staff, every movement relaxed and unhurried, his smile sincere and unforced. 'What do I do when I meet him as his computer expert after Christmas? Keep acting gentle and acquiescent?'

'Obviously. That's if you want to finish what you've started.'

'Oh, I do. When I remember how dreadful Andrea looked... Yes, I *will* do it.'

'He's coming back. Good luck.'

Nan melted away, and Marly softened her features as she turned to face Alex.

Gently he took her elbow and steered her from the room and across the grey and blue carpeted lobby to the entrance, where a chauffeur stood holding open the back door of a silver-grey Mercedes.

Settling in the soft leather seat, she was all too aware of the man close beside her, the spicy scent of his after-shave prickling her nose, the warmth of his body seeming to permeate hers, even though he had made no move to touch her. Watch it, she warned herself. You're supposed to be paying him back for the way he treated Andrea, not falling for him yourself!

'We're dining at the Shangri-la,' he said. 'Is that all right with you?'

'Of course, Mr Hamilton. I'm happy to go wherever you wish to take me.'

He gave her a quick glance, as if not sure whether she was teasing, but her calm stare assured him otherwise, and he gave a little sigh of satisfaction.

'Not Mr Hamilton, Marly, my name is Alex.'

'I couldn't call you that. You are my employer and it wouldn't be seemly.'

'But I'm asking you to do it.'

'No, it is not the custom.'

'I don't believe I'm hearing this,' he muttered.

'I'm sorry if I've offended you.' Putting her palms together, she lowered her head till her chin touched the tops of her fingers in a traditional *wai*. 'I do not wish to make you angry, but——'

'I'm not in the least angry. In fact, I think you're very sweet.'

If only you knew, she thought, doing her best to look demure. 'And I think you're very nice, Mr Hamilton.'

'I hope you'll let me show you just how nice I can be,' he said gruffly.

Beginning to enjoy herself, she gave a laugh, but made no reply.

'We've arrived,' he stated as their car eased up a ramp and came to a stop outside the entrance of the Shangri-la. Not waiting for the chauffeur, he opened his door and hurried round to help her out, cradling her hand in his as he did, and not releasing it.

She could not believe he normally acted this way with his girlfriends, and stifled a giggle at his old-fashioned behaviour.

'May I have my hand back?' she whispered. 'It is not seemly for you to touch me in public.'

'Sorry.' He dropped it fast, but as they entered the vast reception area, milling with people, and a stout man toting a camera backed into her, he automatically cupped his hand under her elbow in a protective gesture, then gave another strangled 'sorry' and let it go.

'In this instance it is quite seemly for you hold my arm, Mr Hamilton,' Marly said, struggling hard not to laugh.

'Then I'll have to make sure we're always in a crowd,' he came back fast, 'because I like the feel of your skin!'

Awarding him full marks for making the most of the situation, Marly glided along beside him. She had been out with many tall men, but there was something about this one that made her feel extra-tiny and helpless. Perhaps it was the aura of invincibility that emanated from him. The divine right of the arrogant male, she supposed, and as she remembered Andrea's tear-stained face, her resolve to give him a taste of his own medicine hardened.

CHAPTER THREE

'WHICH of the Shangri-la restaurants do you fancy going to?' Alex Hamilton asked Marly. 'They have several.'

'I don't know any of them. Thais rarely come here.'

Disconcerted, he stopped in his tracks. 'Why is that? I've only been in Thailand a couple of months, and working flat out at the hotel most of the time, I'm still a stranger to the social scene. If there's any reason why your countrymen don't dine here, we can——'

'Only because we prefer to go where there are fewer tourists.'

Unexpectedly he gave a rich, deep chuckle. 'I'm not doing too well with you, am I? Perhaps we should go outside and begin again?'

About to laugh, she remembered the role she was playing, and said piously, 'Please forgive me, Mr Hamilton, it was rude of me to be so frank.'

'Not at all. I dislike pretence of any kind.'

Oh, he did, did he? Then how would he excuse his dishonesty where Andrea was concerned?

' . . . if that suits you?' he questioned.

Not having heard a word he had said, she nodded and followed him past a huge, perfume-drenched bank of flowers to a lift that took them down to the ground floor and the long, wide terrace that overlooked the lush gardens of the hotel, and the Chao Phraya river that bisected the city.

Small trees, festooned with hundreds of tiny silver lights, illumined a scene of fairy-tale splendour: candle-lit tables, an enormous buffet, some twenty feet long,

filled with assorted cold foods, a dozen or more barbecue carts, each with its chef cooking his own speciality,
be it Tiger Bay prawns, lobsters, poultry or meats, and
white-jacketed waiters staggering under trays laden with
every kind of vegetable.

To Marly, it seemed there wasn't an empty space any-
where, and she happily waited for Alex to be told there
was no room for him. But it was not to be.

'A moment, please, sir.' The *maître d'* himself came
hurrying over. 'We are arranging a table for you.'

As he spoke, two waiters were busy setting one up
beneath a palm tree, and with a flourish he led them to
it. As they sat down, a third waiter came forward with
two glasses and a bottle of champagne in an ice-bucket.

'With the compliments of the Shangri-la, Mr
Hamilton,' the *maître d'* smiled, and bowed away.

'Why are you known here?' Marly asked. 'You told
me you're a stranger in my city.'

'I am. But my face isn't. It's been in your papers and
magazines for weeks.'

'Ah . . . Because of your hotel?'

'Yes.'

'It must make you feel good to be so important.'

He stiffened, as though wondering if she was being
sarcastic, but she fixed him with a wide-eyed stare and
he relaxed.

'It's the job that's important, Marly, not me
personally.'

'But you *are* the job,' she said with pretended naïveté.
'You wouldn't have it if the Riverside didn't belong to
your family.'

He choked on his drink and hurriedly set it down.
'Hamilton Hotels may be a family concern, but we have
a tough board of directors, and no one gets to be in a
top position unless they've proved themselves capable
of handling it.'

'I think you're extremely capable, Mr Hamilton.'

'I can be gentle and caring too, if you'll give me the chance.'

Wishing she could blush to order, Marly lowered her head and tried to look discomfited.

'I've embarrassed you, haven't I?' he went on softly.

'No, but you worry me.'

'Why?'

Keeping her head low to hide the mischief in her eyes, she said, 'Your staff call you a lady-killer.'

'Do they, by God?' His voice was sharp, and she recoiled from him as though nervous. 'What do *you* think?' he asked, softening his tone.

'It isn't seemly for me to comment on the behaviour of my employer.'

'If you had anything nice to say, I think you'd find it very seemly,' came his dry comment. 'Which reminds me, you never did get to tell me what you do at the hotel.'

Here was the moment of truth—well, partial truth, Marly thought and, drawing a deep breath, took the bull by the horns—a singularly apt phrase in the circumstances! 'I'm here to set up a software program for you.'

Astonishment held him silent. '*You* are?' he said finally. 'What's happened to Miss Bradshaw?'

'She was taken ill as she was leaving England, and 3S called and asked me to replace her.'

'I can't believe it.'

'Don't you think me capable?' Marly questioned in her haughtiest manner.

'No, not that. But you seem so young and innocent I can't imagine you in such a high-powered job.'

'I fail to see why. Children of twelve and fourteen can create software packages, and at thirty, in this profession, you are considered over the hill. I'm sure I can do the work as well as Miss Brigshade.'

'Bradshaw,' Alex Hamilton corrected automatically, 'and I'm sure you can too. It's just that you took me by surprise. Do you work for 3S or are you a freelance?'

'I'm a freelance,' Marly replied. '3S were put in touch with me by my friend Nan, who also works at your hotel. I live with her and her family.'

'I see.'

Glad that he didn't, she searched for a means of changing the subject. 'I hope you won't consider me rude, Mr Hamilton, but I'm very hungry.'

'Good heavens! How remiss of me. I'm so interested in knowing more about you that I forgot about food. Do you want to order from the menu or try the buffet?'

'The buffet, please.' Rising, she glided towards the long table, Alex following on her heels. Here, the food was cold, each dish and tureen so wonderfully decorated that it could have been framed and hung on a wall. 'Don't you think it looks too good to eat, Mr Hamilton?'

'I can't tell. My eyes are blinded by *you*.'

'Are you usually so complimentary to the women you take out?'

'Yes. But until tonight, I've never meant it!'

Biting back the urge to tell him that this line was so old it had cobwebs hanging from it, she gave him a gentle smile instead, and he instantly smiled back. As if it were an actual radiance enveloping her, her body grew hot and her limbs trembled. Watch it, she warned herself. This man is dangerous and not to be taken seriously.

Quickly skirting the buffet, she headed for a barbecue cart serving an assortment of shellfish. She was careful not to look directly at Alex Hamilton, though a swift glance showed he was studying the food served by each cart, and she wondered if the same things would be featured on the Riverside menu before the week was out. Smiling at the thought, she watched him, noting how thick and dark his lashes were, and how the deep cleft in his firm chin saved it from hardness. As he bent towards the chef who was filling his plate with slivers of barbecued meats and stuffed chicken wings, a tawny lock of hair fell on his forehead, and she experienced a strong urge to touch it and see if it was as silky as it appeared.

Annoyed with herself, she picked up her plate and returned to their table, and as she did, common sense reasserted itself. It wasn't surprising she was responding to Alex Hamilton's blatant good looks. After all, dozens—maybe hundreds—of girls had already done the same, and in that respect she was no different. But where the difference lay was the manner in which she responded to the man himself. And since she despised his morals and was disgusted by his lack of principle, there was no fear of her falling for him.

Alex joined her, a waiter following with a tray stacked with food. Her eyes widened at the amount but she said nothing.

'I noticed you only took a few Tiger Bay prawns,' he commented, settling opposite her. 'I wasn't sure if well brought-up Thai ladies don't consider it good form to eat too much in public, or whether you were too shy because you work for me, so I thought I'd tempt you with a few more dishes.'

She was touched by his thoughtfulness, until she realised it was part and parcel of his armoury for disarming his prey before going in for the kill.

'How kind you are,' she simpered. 'And you were right.'

'Which one was the reason?'

'Both!'

'A pity,' he drawled. 'That will make it doubly difficult for me to get to know you.' He paused. 'Difficult, but I hope not impossible.'

Hiding the thrill of triumph that shot through her, she began to eat. 'My father says hope is one of the most important emotions a person can have.'

'Your father sounds a man after my own heart. Does he live in the city?'

'Not at present. He and my mother are in Dallas for a year. My father's a lawyer with an oil company.' At least that part of her story was true, which meant one lie less to remember.

'So that's why you're living with Nan,' Alex Hamilton said. 'Wouldn't you have preferred to live on your own?'

Did she detect a note of regret in his voice that his evening with her wasn't going to end up in her bed? Hiding her amusement, she decided to give him a few other things to mull over.

'Thai children rarely leave home until they marry— and not always then, if the parental house is large enough.'

'Wouldn't you prefer to have your own place?'

'Why should I? I have no desire to have an affair, and living with my family is far more convenient.'

Startled grey eyes met hers. 'For a shy young lady, you can be remarkably frank.'

'We see nothing wrong in talking honestly about our feelings.'

'Only talking?'

Deliberately she stared him full in the face. 'I am a virgin, Mr Hamilton, if that is what you are asking.'

'I—I——' Flummoxed, he stopped, his heightened colour showing that again she had taken him by surprise.

'When will you have time to discuss the software programs you want me to do?' she asked before he could recover. 'I'm bored doing nothing.'

'If I'd known *you* were waiting for me,' he replied, his wits returning, 'I'd have seen you the instant I got back! Beats me why my secretary didn't tell me Miss Bradshaw wasn't able to come. I——'

'I'd like to start earning my salary,' Marly cut in, intent on showing him she was uninterested in further flattery. 'I assume you'll want the software in Thai as well as English?'

'Yes, but concentrate on the English version first, so I can make sure it covers everything I want, before you start on the translation.'

'I'll bring in someone else to do that,' she said quickly. 'Your requirements will be complicated enough to require several programs, and a translator can start on one while I'm devising another.' Suddenly aware she sounded too assured, Marly gave a nervous cough. 'If that meets with your approval, of course?'

'Everything you say meets with my approval, other than your refusal to use my first name.' Spoon and fork poised to help himself to a succulent mix of chicken and baby aubergine, each one no bigger than a walnut, he gave her the full battery of his deep grey eyes. 'Can't you forget tradition and call me Alex? After all, I call you Marly.'

'You're my employer.'

'Who wants to be your friend. Come on, say it,' he cajoled.

Fluttering her lashes at him, she whispered his name.

'There,' he said, satisfied. 'That wasn't too painful, was it?'

'No, Mr Ha—Alex.' She tilted her head towards him. 'I've never met an Alex before.'

'And I've never met a Marly.' He began to eat. 'That bodes well for us.'

'Why?'

'Because we don't have any preconceived associations with each other's names. If you'd been called Sandra, I'd have had a problem. She was the first girl I fell in love with—I was fourteen at the time—and she broke my heart.'

'You mean she turned you down?'

'Worse. She called me fat and spotty!'

For the first time Marly's laugh was genuine. 'How long did it take you to recover?'

'As long as it took me to become spotless and skinny!' A well shaped hand, the fingers long and artistic, rubbed the side of his face. 'I suppose that with your Thai passion for honesty you'd have said the same as she did?'

'Never.' Marly quickly slipped back into the role she was playing. 'We are taught to be frank without being hurtful.'

'Does that mean that when I ask to see you again you'll turn me down politely?'

'I'll always be polite.'

'And always turn me down?'

'It depends how busy I am. I'm only contracted to work for you for two months, and we've already wasted ten days of it.' Primly she regarded him. 'Will you be going away again soon?'

'Not as far as I know. I'm here for six months—until all the bugs are ironed out and the hotel is running smoothly. Then I move on to wherever I'm needed.'

'Are you what they call a trouble-shot?'

'A trouble-shooter,' he corrected, his grin making him look younger than the thirty-four she knew him to be.

'Do you normally travel a lot?' she asked, hoping to lead him into discussing his stay in Singapore.

'Yes. For the past two years I've moved between the Far East and Australia.'

'Where were you before you came to Thailand?'

'Sydney, Tokyo, Hong Kong, Singapore——'

'I'd love to go to Singapore,' she interjected. 'Did you like it?'

'It isn't my favourite place,' he answered flatly. 'I prefer Bali and——'

'Why don't you like it?' she persisted.

'I had an unpleasant experience there that left a rather sour taste.'

What a hateful way of describing Andrea! A sour taste! 'Is it anything you can discuss?' she asked, oozing sympathy.

'If I did, you'd find it extremely boring.' He raked a hand through his tawny hair, as if trying to throw off the memory of it. 'Anyway, why waste this lovely setting talking of unpleasant things when we could be talking about *you*?' He leaned towards her, his chiselled features softened by desire. 'Do you have a boyfriend, Marly?'

'No,' she replied truthfully.

'It has to be from choice. I can't believe no man has wanted you.'

'I've never met one *I* wanted.' Until I saw *you* walking across the lobby, she thought, though the feeling had died when she had discovered how heartless he was. But none of her thoughts was apparent on her face as she met his gaze. 'I believe marriage is for life, Mr Hamilton, and I will have to be absolutely certain about a man before I commit myself to him.'

'How young you sound,' Alex stated, a long-fingered hand playing with the stem of his wine glass. 'When you're my age you'll know nothing is certain in life.'

Except for one thing, Marly knew: her determination to cut this man down to size.

'I'm surprised to hear you say that,' she said dulcetly, 'because in the last hour I've become very certain of *you*.'

Beautifully marked eyebrows arched above smoky grey eyes. 'Now that's an intriguing statement. Care to explain it?'

She nodded. 'I'm certain you have a strong sense of honour; that you never wittingly break your word, and that you respect the feelings and wishes of anyone you care for.' Her lids lowered and thick black lashes, long and straight as a doll's, fanned her cheeks as she prepared to deliver the final blow. 'I'm also certain you will respect my wish to remain untouched until I marry. Only on that basis am I willing to see you again, should you do me the honour of asking me.'

Alex leaned back in his chair, his body motionless, his face so devoid of expression that she wondered if she had gone too far. The intention was to intrigue him by being different from his previous girlfriends, not frighten him off completely! Around her she was aware of waiters moving, diners leaving, the clink of glasses, the throb of a passing river boat, the splutter of the pink candle glowing between herself and the man opposite her.

'Marly, I...' His voice was husky. 'I wouldn't be doing you an honour to ask you out. You'd be doing *me* the honour by accepting. And I will always respect your wishes. You can trust me completely.'

As a chicken could trust a fox! she thought, but blinked her lashes and glowed at him. 'Thank you for saying that.'

'My pleasure.' He raised his glass to her. 'No more worries, eh? Any change of mind will have to come from you.'

His strategy was as clear as if he had handed it to her on a sheet of paper. She could see every move. Romantic dinners in glamorous places, the serious conversations, the light wine, the chaste goodnight kisses... Until one night when they would dine alone in his suite, and the talk would be more sensuous than serious, the wine heady, the kisses deep and drugging... So drugging that she would be begging him to make love to her. What a swine he was!

Furiously she flung out her arm and the glass in front of her shattered to the floor.

Startled, Alex jumped to his feet and came round to her. 'Marly! What's wrong?'

Bemused, she stared at him, then shook her head. 'An insect, I think. It bit me.' With an effort she gathered herself together. 'I'm sorry I startled you.'

'Are you sure you're all right?'

'A little tired perhaps.'

'Then I'll take you home.'

Within moments they were in the Mercedes. Alex made no attempt to move close to her, but she was intensely conscious of his tall frame in the confines of the car, and carefully looked away from him, relieved that he seemed content to sit in silence.

'When may I see you again?' he asked as the car stopped outside the timbered house and he escorted her to the locked gates leading into the compound surrounding it.

'In the hotel,' she replied, stepping into the courtyard as the family's night-watchman unbolted the gate.

'That isn't what I meant.'

'I know.'

With a laugh she lifted her long skirt and ran gracefully up the steps and into the house, firmly resisting the urge to turn and see if he was watching her. But the instant she closed the door, she peered through the peephole and saw he was still standing by the gate, a tall, wide-shouldered figure exuding a power and purpose that would brook no denial.

Yet deny him she would, and enjoy herself immensely in the process.

CHAPTER FOUR

NAN almost choked herself laughing when Marly told her that Alex Hamilton had treated her as though she were a fragile piece of china.

'When are you going to give him his come-uppance and tell him you've made a fool of him?' she asked when she could finally speak.

'Not until he's fallen for me good and hard.'

'I hope you can keep up the butter-wouldn't-melt-in-your-mouth act?'

'That's the only problem. A few times this evening I almost forgot myself and verbally slew him!'

'If you wore Thai clothes it might remind you to curb your tongue! I'll lend you some of my cheong-sams,' Nan encouraged.

'Do you think I should wear them the whole time?'

'Well, women staff at the hotel do, though I suppose you could change when you're off-duty. Except that you were wearing one when he first saw you, and that might be part of your attraction.'

'Won't the staff find it strange if they see me pretending to be Thai?'

'Not if you say you're doing it to play a joke on someone. Then they'll never give you away.'

Apart from a great sense of humour, Thais were among the most generous people on earth, Marly mused one morning after Christmas as she riffled through the brocades, silks and cottons Nan had placed in her wardrobe. Even though she knew cotton was cooler for day wear,

she plumped for a peach silk, its long narrow skirt slit
up the side to facilitate walking, the tight-fitting, short-
sleeved top cut short to show an intriguing two-inch expanse of skin between top and skirt. It was a more con-
stricting outfit than her normal casual summer wear, but
needs must when the goal she hoped to achieve was going
to give her so much satisfaction.

She reminded herself of this as she touched eyeliner
to her chestnut-brown eyes, and centre-parted her hair
for it to fall sleek and straight to below her shoulders.

If my family saw me now, she thought humorously,
they'd walk right by me!

She proved this conclusively when a security guard
she had seen for the past seven days stopped her and
asked whom she wished to see as she crossed the hotel
lobby and mounted the stairs to the mezzanine floor and
offices. Hiding a smile, she answered him in Thai, telling
him who she was.

His astonishment was gratifying, and in a conspira-
torial whisper she fed him the story Nan had suggested.
He chuckled and slapped his thigh, and enjoining him
to warn his colleagues to keep her secret, she went into
her office.

The air-conditioning kept the Riverside comfortably
cool, yet despite this she found working in a cheong-
sam too warm, and was wondering how to make herself
comfortable when Alex Hamilton strode in, thick, tawny
hair ruthlessly brushed flat, though an errant strand in
the front was beginning to curl.

Gracefully she rose, placed her palms together, and
waied him.

'Don't do that to me,' he said instantly. 'It isn't
necessary.'

'We always greet our superiors this way.'

'I'm not your superior; I'm your employer.'

'You are playing with words, Mr Hamilton.'

'You agreed to call me Alex.'

'Not in the office. It wouldn't be seemly.'

'Now how did I know you were going to say that?' he smiled, coming to stand directly in front of her. 'I must be psychic!' Wood-smoke eyes ranged slowly over her as if committing her to memory. 'Since we met, I haven't been able to stop thinking of you.'

Many men had said the same to her, but none had made her heart beat faster, as it was now doing, and she wondered if it was because of the intensity of his gaze, as if she was the only woman in his world worth concentrating on. But then he was the sort of man who would do everything with intensity: loving and hating, working or playing. And playing the field too, she thought grimly. Like it or not, he was a born heart-breaker.

'Have you been thinking of *me*?' he broke into her thoughts.

'Oh, yes.' He looked delighted, and she added prosaically, 'I've been working out the software you will require, and I'd like to discuss my ideas with you.'

'I've more than a few ideas for you myself,' he quipped, the smile on his lips dying as she froze him with a look.

'Please don't make it embarrassing for me to work with you, Mr Hamilton, or I'll have to ask 3S to find a replacement.'

'Are you always such a stickler for protocol?'

'We are brought up to believe in it.' Marly pretended to hesitate, then said diffidently, 'You may find it interesting to read a book on our customs. There are several good ones available.'

'I'll ask my secretary to get them all! It won't do me any good if I keep offending you!'

'You haven't offended me. I always make allowances for people.'

His startled expression showed he was unused to being put in his place, and she hoped she hadn't overplayed her hand. But the wry smile he gave her was reassuring, and she glided over to her desk, wondering how to appear gentle and shy while talking high technology. It was going to be tricky but she had to manage it.

'While I was waiting for you to return from abroad,' she said, careful to keep her voice soft, 'I prepared a questionnaire I would like each hotel guest to fill in when they arrive.'

'What sort of questions?'

For answer, she took a four-page folder from the drawer of her desk and gave it to him.

Raising an eyebrow in surprise at the size of it, he perched on the side of her desk to peruse it. From beneath her thick, straight lashes, she studied him. This morning he was formally dressed in a dark business suit—the only concession to the tropical climate being its lightweight material.

It was the first occasion she had seen him close up in daylight, and not even the bright sunlight could find a flaw in the symmetry of his features. Indeed he was so preposterously handsome that he might have been thought effeminate, were it not for the firmness of the wide, sensual mouth, the imperiousness of the long, firm nose, and the strength in the well defined eyebrows, several shades darker than the tawny hair swept back from his high forehead.

'This questionnaire is very in-depth,' he commented, raising his head. 'I'm impressed.'

'Thank you. If I know the likes and dislikes of everyone who stays here, I can devise software to help you solve any problems that may arise with food, recreational facilities, bedroom requirements and——'

'Bedroom requirements?' His mouth quirked, though his voice remained serious.

'Yes, Mr Hamilton.' Her voice was as serious as his. 'Some guests dislike room service entering their suite, others object to their beds being turned down, and when it comes to air-conditioning, your staff say the complaints are legion.'

'And how! We've even had requests for duvets. Duvets in the tropics,' he reiterated. 'They must be bloody mad!'

Deliberately she flinched, and he stopped short. 'Anything wrong?'

'I'm not used to obscenities.'

'I'd hardly call bl——' He stopped abruptly. 'Sorry.'

'I accept your apology,' she said primly, wondering how he'd react if she repeated some of her brothers' colourful language.

'I don't believe your fellow countrymen never swear,' Alex muttered.

'Only when they lose their temper. But you hadn't. You were merely expressing a thought aggressively.'

She hid a grin as chagrin darted across his face, and silently applauded herself for making him feel uncomfortable. 'Forgive me for commenting on your behaviour, Mr Hamilton. You're my superior and——'

'Not that again,' he cut in. 'And stop this "Mr" nonsense. When we're alone, it's Alex.'

Afraid she had annoyed him, she smiled at him tentatively, and the way he studied her mouth gave her the assurance she required. Alex Hamilton might have a love 'em and leave 'em reputation, but right now he was definitely at the love 'em stage!

'May we continue our business discussion?' she asked.

'By all means. But first you should realise that most luxury hotels offer the same facilities we do, but where I believe *we* can score points is by making our guests feel at home.'

'How?'

'By ensuring that the second time they stay in one of our hotels, that hotel knows their foibles *before* they arrive; that way we can put their favourite drinks and flowers in their room, the reception clerk can enquire about their children or their wife——'

'Whether they prefer morning coffee to tea,' Marly cut in, 'or bath-towels to robes! That's easy. All I need do is enlarge the questionnaire.'

'How long before you can let us have the software?'

'It depends on the problems I come across.'

Alex's mouth crooked in a half-smile. 'I suppose it's part of your job to make it sound complex. How else could 3S justify their fee?'

'If you think I'd be party to such a——'

'I was teasing,' he said quickly. 'I've no idea of their charges. That's our finance director's province.'

'I see.' Her annoyance, which was genuine, faded. 'I'm sorry I misunderstood you.'

'Misunderstandings seem par for our course.'

'I agree.' She paused deliberately before continuing. 'For that reason, it would be better if we didn't see each other socially.'

'You're joking?' The astonishment on his face told her no female had ever said such a thing to him. 'I thought you liked me.'

'I do.'

'Then why——?'

'Because it will create problems.'

'How?'

'Do you often date your staff?'

'No. This is a first.'

'Why are you making an exception of *me*?'

'Because you're an exceptional young woman.'

'Exceptional?' Wide-eyed, she gazed at him, and he lowered his head towards her so that she saw the silver flecks in his grey eyes.

'You are intelligent, charming, and very feminine.'

'So are thousands of other women.'

'But *you* don't flaunt your intelligence.'

In other words I'm docile, Marly thought, and knew her plan was succeeding. He had probably dated intelligent women by the hundred, but one who also deferred to him constantly was a novelty not to be lightly discarded! Slowly she turned away, affording him a view of her small, straight nose and sweetly curved mouth.

'Are you always embarrassed by compliments?' he quizzed.

'If they come from my employer.'

'Can't you just see me as a man who wants to know you better?'

Certain that he meant 'know' in the biblical sense, Marly longed to cut him down to size, but knowing this would put paid to her plans for him, she swallowed her ire and gave him one of her shy smiles.

'No comment?' he ventured.

'It wouldn't be seemly.'

'I bet I'm going to hear *that* pretty often!' He leaned closer to her. 'Are you free to have dinner with me tonight?'

'I have another engagement,' she lied.

'Tomorrow, then?'

His persistence was gratifying, but she had no intention of making it easy for him. Let him sweat a little!

'I'm sorry, but I promised Nan's mother I would be home to dinner.'

'Have a drink with me beforehand?'

'Thank you.'

'I'll call for you here and we'll go up to the Rivertop. We promote it as having the best view and the best cocktails in Bangkok, and I'd like to see how honest our advertising is!'

As the door shut behind him, Marly danced a little jig around the room. Her long, tight skirt hampered her and she sat down giggling, and stared at her blank computer screen. Blank? Then why was Alex Hamilton's face filling it? She poked her tongue at it and the image vanished.

Although she had no regrets about her charade, she knew that by encouraging him to fall in love with her she was playing a dangerous game. He was the handsomest, most interesting man she had met, and if she wasn't careful she could emulate Andrea and, she suspected, every other woman with whom he came in contact, and fall madly in love with him.

Yet she had one advantage. She knew the man behind the mask. Not for her the rose-coloured spectacles of innocence. She saw him for the philanderer he was, and that should be enough to keep her immune to him.

So absorbed was she in thought that the telephone rang twice before she heard it. It was Kevin, to see if she was free to go to the cinema with him that evening. Glad the engagement she had pretended to have was now an actuality, she accepted at once. Besides, it would be a relief to be herself again.

'What are we seeing?' she asked.

'The new Spielberg. It's the opening night, and I've unexpectedly been given two tickets. I'll pick you up at seven-thirty.'

An evening with a nice uncomplicated man would help her put Alex into perspective, and remind her he wasn't the *only* handsome male in the world. Except that Kevin, attractive though he was, left her cold. On the credit side, though, she couldn't envisage him two-timing anyone, and that, as far as she was concerned, was a great big plus.

CHAPTER FIVE

RETURNING home to shower and change, Marly wished Nan wasn't working late, for they both enjoyed their pre-dinner gossip, and right now she had plenty to gossip about!

She was dressed and ready half an hour before Kevin was due, and enjoyed wearing her own clothes. She had gone slightly overboard, with citron and white linen a dramatic contrast against her olive skin, and the smooth sleekness of her centre-parted hairstyle had been replaced by her usual one of tonged curls cascading to her shoulders.

'Here comes the Marly I recognise!' Nan's mother exclaimed as the girl she had seen grow from a tomboy into a beautiful woman entered the living-room, high-heeled sandals clicking on the polished wood floor. 'I take it you aren't seeing Mr Hamilton tonight?'

'Thank heavens, no. It's an awful strain pretending to be a docile young lady and agreeing with everything he says.'

'There's no reason why you can't disagree with him,' the older woman stated. 'In the last ten years my countrywomen have become much more emancipated, and many of them run big companies and are highly successful.'

'Alex hasn't realised that, so I'm still playing up to his outmoded ideas!'

'He'll change them when he's lived here a little longer.'

Marly knew this to be true, for the twentieth century, with its satellite television and world-wide communication, was having the same impact here as in the West. Yet family bonds were still important, religion remained strong, and young people continued to treat their parents with respect.

Professor Damrong came in, and watching him greet his wife—smiling without touching, the smile itself being an embrace—Marly thought it a nicer salutation than the meaningless peck on the cheek of a Western couple.

A few moments later Kevin arrived, and after a drink and the usual social chat they set off for the cinema.

'The professor was telling me what a success the show was,' he commented as they strolled down the street in search of a cab. 'I wish I could have seen your act.'

Marly almost told him she was still acting, then decided against it. Alex Hamilton was occupying enough of her thoughts without allowing him to impinge on her evening with Kevin.

An empty cab cruised past and he flagged it down and ushered her inside. But they had only gone a few blocks when she asked the driver to stop.

'I think we'll be better off walking the rest of the way,' she suggested. 'This traffic jam is dreadful.'

'Suits me.' Kevin paid the fare and helped her out. 'As long as your high heels are up to it!'

'It isn't my heels that worry me,' she laughed, 'it's the heat. How did the world manage before the invention of air-conditioning?'

'With difficulty! If I'd been born a hundred years ago I'd have moved to Iceland.'

'You'll be happy as a sandboy when you're in the cinema,' Marly assured him. 'They generally keep the temperature Siberian!'

He laughed and caught her hand, not letting it go until they reached their destination.

Having been to the cinema often during her visits to Bangkok, Marly was unsurprised by their size and décor.

Thai cinemas were a throw-back to the large, lavishly decorated ones of the forties and fifties.

The huge foyer was crowded, and as Kevin squeezed a path for them through the throng, some instinct made her look sharply to her left.

Oh, no! Dismayed, she stared at a dark gold head towering above all the other ones. Just her bad luck that Alex Hamilton was here! Any second now he would turn and see her as her real self. She ducked behind a large woman, wondering if Kevin would notice if she bent her knees and mimicked the walk of Groucho Marx! Of course there was always the hope that in this crush Alex wouldn't spot her, and if their seats weren't near each other... Yet it wasn't a chance she was prepared to take. If they didn't come face to face now, it might still happen in the interval or as they went out!

'You OK?' Kevin asked.

'Yes.' She thought quickly. 'I want to go to the powder-room before we sit down.'

'I'll wait for you here.'

Keeping her head low, she weaved through the crowds, breathing a sigh of relief as she entered the cloakroom.

A gaggle of giggling girls monopolised the mirror that lined one wall and, deciding against redoing her hair in front of an audience, Marly went into a toilet cubicle to do it.

She was trembling, and she stood quietly for a moment, chiding herself for getting in such a state. Heavens! The worst that could happen was that Alex Hamilton would see her as she was and wonder why she had embarked on her charade, and it wouldn't be much of a problem to come up with a satisfactory reason.

But the image of Andrea's gaunt face revived her fighting spirit, and with steady hands she took a small hairbrush from her bag and, with fierce strokes, brushed out the curls until her hair was as nature had intended;

then she carefully parted it in the centre and combed it down either side of her face. Instantly her face was transformed, the gamine beauty giving way to a serene one.

Unfortunately there was nothing she could do about her dress; amusingly sexy when worn by Amalia Bradshaw, it was incongruous—and all the more startling—when worn by smooth-haired, gently mannered Marly. She hitched the low neckline as high as possible, but it still showed a lot of cleavage... Oh, well, she had done the best she could. Snapping shut her bag, she hurried out to Kevin, interested to see what he would make of her transformation.

The foyer was emptying rapidly, giving him a good look at her as she came towards him.

'Why the quick change?' he questioned. 'And what for?'

'*Who* for?' she corrected, and waited until they were seated—breathing easier when she glimpsed Alex Hamilton some distance in front of her—before explaining to Kevin what she had meant. 'I'm playing a joke on my boss. He's here and I didn't want him to see me *au naturel*. I'll fill you in properly later.'

'I'll hold you to that,' Kevin said, still bemused. 'There's more drama being with you than on the screen!'

She made a face at him and he chuckled as they settled back to enjoy the film.

Though it was an entertaining piece of escapism, Marly's thoughts centred on Alex. Was he here because like herself he was a Spielberg fan, or because it was the right place to be seen? She knew so little about him, and wished she'd had more time to question Andrea. She had half a mind to write and tell her what she was doing, but decided against it. Time enough to do so when Alex had bitten the dust.

Two hours later, as the final credits faded from the screen, she moved slowly up the aisle. Though there was now no reason for Alex not to see her, inexplicably she still wanted to avoid him, but it was not to be, for he was chatting in the foyer to a European couple, beside him a young and pretty blonde. Across her head he glimpsed Marly, and murmuring something to the girl, he sauntered towards her.

'Hello, Marly,' he said. 'This is an unexpected pleasure.'

Composedly she *waied* him, irritably aware how insignificant he made all other men appear. A beige suit emphasised his height and wide shoulders, the pale colour heightening the bronze tan of his skin and drawing attention to his thick, tawny hair. There was no doubt he was a lion of a man and, like the king of the jungle, had the same air of confidence and supremacy.

He was as aware of her as she was of him, for his eyes ranged openly over her, surprise apparent in their grey depths as they took in her swirling skirt and shoe-string-tied top that revealed as much as it concealed.

'Did you enjoy the film?' he asked.

'Very much,' she said composedly. 'Did you?'

He nodded, simultaneously glancing at Kevin, and she introduced them.

'Why don't you both join me for supper?' Alex suggested, his eyes skimming her body again.

'We've already booked a table somewhere,' she said before Kevin could speak.

'Another time, then,' he murmured, and half raising his hand, returned to his friends.

Marly gave a sigh of relief. 'Thank goodness he didn't persist.'

'Not likely after the brush-off you gave him,' Kevin observed as they inched their way through the foyer.

'It wasn't a brush-off. I just said we'd already made plans. He wasn't to know I was lying.'

'He's not the type to take it kindly if he found out.'

'It would just be a case of the biter being bit. Compared with him, Benedict Arnold was honest!'

'It's time you explained yourself, old girl. But first, why did you suddenly change nationalities this evening?'

'I'll tell you at dinner,' she promised. 'I'm too hungry to think of anything else.'

'Where shall we go?' he asked as they set off down the road, the evening as warm as an English heatwave. 'Do you fancy Thai or Western food?'

'If you'd care for Chinese,' she suggested, 'I know just the place.'

'Lead on!'

'Crawl on,' she quipped, for the pavements were so crowded that one could only move at a snail's pace.

Only when they turned down a side-street was it quieter, though small, dimly lit dressmaker and tailor shops were still open.

'Beats me the long hours they keep,' Kevin muttered.

'It's tough for anyone who caters for the tourist trade,' Marly stated. 'Though hotels bear the brunt of it.'

Catching his arm, she stopped in front of the dimmest shop in the narrow turning, and ignoring his dubious expression, led the way through a dreary, white-tiled interior to a charming, candlelit courtyard beyond. She saw instantly that the dozen or so tables were all occupied, though at sight of her a rotund Chinese hurried across and greeted her like a long-lost friend, clearly remembering her from the two evenings she had eaten here with Nan.

'This is Mr Wong,' she said, introducing him to Kevin. 'He makes the best Peking duck in the world.'

Beaming at the compliment, Mr Wong hastily summoned a waiter to set up an extra table, and moments later she and Kevin, seated in a recessed area of the courtyard, were devouring crisp fried seaweed and bite-size spring rolls as they waited for their main course.

'I'm still waiting to hear why you're playing a joke on your boss,' Kevin reminded her.

Marly considered whether to lie—after all, Andrea's misery was not for public ears—then decided to give him a monitored version. Yet even monitored, Alex came out of it badly, though surprisingly Kevin stuck up for him.

'You've only heard your friend's side of the story,' he warned. 'Wouldn't you say that one good thing in Hamilton's favour is that he was honest enough to say he no longer loved her?'

'He proposed marriage.'

'People do fall out of love, you know. And surely it's better to admit it before you slip on the ring, rather than after?'

'Put like that, yes,' Marly agreed. 'But the man's an out-and-out swine. He had no intention of marrying Andrea. He fancied her and stopped at nothing to get her into bed.'

'Women can be pretty ruthless too,' Kevin said drily, the tightening of his mouth indicating it was more than simply a passing comment.

'Have I touched a sore point?' Marly asked.

'It's healed now.'

'But you still don't want to talk about it.' It was a statement rather than a question.

Unexpectedly he laughed. 'But *you* would, wouldn't you, Miss Nosy Parker?'

'I'm not nosy,' she protested, 'just curious.'

'Same thing. Anyway, I've no objection to telling you. I fell for a girl in medical school and we planned to marry when we qualified. Unfortunately she married someone else.'

'You didn't blame Alex Hamilton for changing *his* mind,' she pointed out.

'The difference is that Jenny turned me down for a highly successful plastic surgeon twenty-five years her senior!'

'Seems to me you had a lucky escape.'

'I know, but it soured me.' His mouth curved upwards. 'I'm getting sweeter by the minute, though.'

'Not over me, I hope.' She deemed it wiser to be frank, particularly in view of what he had just told her.

'I *was* hoping,' he admitted.

'Please don't. I'm not on the market.'

'Is there someone else?'

'No.' Well, there wasn't, she told herself; merely a fleeting hope that Andrea had unwittingly extinguished. 'I'm just here for a short time,' she said aloud, 'and I'm not interested in any emotional involvements.'

'May we meet as friends?'

'I'd like that. It's just that I didn't want to go out with you under false pretences.'

Kevin gave a shout of laughter. 'You're only false with Alex Hamilton, I take it?'

She gave a wry smile. 'Do you think it's mean of me playing this joke on him?'

Kevin took a moment to answer. 'Not as long as it remains a joke,' he said finally. 'Don't play him for a fool, Marly. He could be a bad loser.'

'I'll bear that in mind,' she promised, and was glad of the arrival of their crisp and luscious duck, which precluded further discussion of the man she most wanted to talk about, but wouldn't.

CHAPTER SIX

TOSSING in her bed that night, Marly acknowledged she was far more vulnerable to Alex Hamilton's sexual magnetism than was wise, and wished she hadn't agreed to have a drink with him the following evening. Yet if she didn't see him socially she would not be able to bring about his emotional downfall, and since this was the crux of her plan she had no option but to make herself available. Angrily she pummelled her pillow, and when she finally fell asleep, it was to dream that she was pummelling Alex's chest.

In the morning, heavy-eyed, she frowned at her face in the bathroom mirror. A few more restless nights like the last one, and the bags under her eyes would be large enough to put shopping in! Then, instead of wanting to get close to her, Alex would be off and running. A man of his calibre would never be attracted to a woman unless she was beautiful.

'Not that you're beautiful,' Marly said to her reflection. 'But in the role you're playing you're certainly different from his usual girlfriends.'

An hour later, showered and dressed in a cheongsam—a peacock-blue cotton this time—she headed for the hotel and another meeting with Alex to try to finalise the program she was devising.

Entering his office, she found him seated in a black leather chair behind his desk, and had to steel herself against the devastating smile that lit up his fine-boned face. Watch it, old girl, the objective is to make him fall in love with you for Andrea's sake, not so you can have him for yourself!

Greeting him with her customary *wai*, she extracted a sheaf of papers from the file she had brought with her, and handed them to him. 'I've outlined the program I think you need, Mr Hamilton,' she said demurely. 'If you could spare the time to read it...'

'Right away,' he smiled. 'And when we're alone you promised to call me Alex.'

Acknowledging this by a movement of her head, she modestly lowered her eyes and waited for him to study the document she had given him.

'Excellent,' he commented after several moments. 'You've obviously given these questions great thought.'

She fluttered her lashes at him, aware of his graceful long fingers raking back a tawny lock of hair from his forehead. How would those fingers feel on her skin? Banishing the treacherous thought, she concentrated on what he was saying.

'There are several more questions I wish to add,' he went on, and picking up a gold pen from his desk, wrote them down in a strong, flowing hand. 'See if you agree,' he said, scanning her face as he handed her back the questionnaire.

Marly read through his additions and nodded. 'We're clearly on the same wavelength.'

'I hope that will apply to more than business,' he said, and leaning back in his chair added deliberately, 'Did you enjoy yourself last night?'

'Very much.'

'Where did you eat?'

'At a little place we found last time,' she said, awarding herself top marks for adding 'last time'.

'You know Kevin Rossiter well, then?'

'Quite well.' Triumph coursed through her. He sounded jealous, which was great. Inclining her head, she glided towards the door.

'How did you meet him?' The deep voice stopped her in her tracks and she glanced over her shoulder.

'He works at the hospital with Professor Damrong—Nan's father.'

Alex opened his mouth and shut it again—as if thinking better of pursuing the subject. 'I'll see you to-night,' he said, and with a lithe movement came round the side of the desk to open the door for her.

Marly spent the remainder of the day photocopying the revised questionnaire and distributing it to the guests. Because she was so busy she turned down Nan's invitation to lunch with her in the coffee-shop, and had a sandwich delivered to her office.

At six-fifteen, exhausted but satisfied with the progress she had made, she went to the cloakroom to freshen her make-up and tidy her hair. She had caught it back from her face with a wide tortoiseshell slide, but now she let it fall free to her shoulders, aware that it made her appear considerably younger, though this might also be due to the added sparkle in her eyes and the pink flush in her cheeks. She was as excited as a teenager at the prospect of going out again with Alex, and firmly told herself it was because her plan was proceeding the way she wanted.

Returning to her office, she found him waiting for her. He had changed from his formal grey business suit to white linen trousers and unstructured jacket, with a black sports shirt, open-necked to show tanned skin and a smattering of bronze hair.

Silently he took her arm and steered her towards the glass-encased lift. Although her body tingled at the pressure of his hand she managed to hide it, determined not to give him the satisfaction of knowing how physically aware of him she was.

The revolving roof-top tower afforded a stupendous view of Bangkok and the river, and though she and Nan had treated themselves to drinks here while she had been waiting for Alex to return from abroad, she pretended she was seeing it for the first time and was entranced.

'It's unbelievable,' she breathed. 'I've never seen anything so lovely.'

'Nor have I,' he admitted, staring at Marly. 'I've been looking forward to this all day.'

'I can't imagine why,' she said with artless innocence. 'I'm not as sophisticated as your girlfriends.'

'Thank heavens for that! If I——'

He broke off as a waiter came over to lead them to a table by the window, the only one unoccupied. A bottle of champagne in an ice-bucket stood on it, with two fluted glasses, and he signalled the waiter to fill them.

'To us,' Alex toasted her, raising his glass.

Uncertain how to reply, she remained silent. Nan, of course, would have made some witty response, but then she had had the benefit—if benefit it could be called—of a British boarding-school education, while she herself was pretending she had been raised in the traditional manner. Lowering her lids as if shy, she sipped the bubbling liquid. She was no expert on champagne, but the mellow biscuity taste told her this was one of the best, and sight of the Cristal label confirmed it. Alex was sparing no expense to please her—or did he treat all his women with the same largesse? Somehow the champagne no longer tasted vintage, and she abruptly set down her glass.

'Anything wrong?' he asked instantly.

'I am embarrassed by your extravagance towards me. I'm happy to be with you even if we drink only water.'

'I appreciate you saying so.' His voice was serious though she sensed his amusement. 'But I can afford the best and that's what I'd always want for you.'

In which case you should get out of my life, Marly thought silently, recollecting the lies he had fabricated to seduce Andrea. Behind them came the tinkling of a piano playing tunes from the Thirties, which seemed to go well with the elegant art deco furnishings, and she forced her bitter thoughts away in case they reflected on her face and set him pondering. Intrigued by her though he appeared to be, Alex was nobody's fool and she would do well to remember it.

'Have dinner with me tonight,' he said suddenly.

'I can't. I told you I promised to have it at home with Professor Damrong and Khun Ladda.'

'Khun Ladda?' he queried.

'The professor's wife. Khun is our equivalent of your "Mrs", and Ladda is her maiden name.'

'You mean she isn't really married to the professor?' Alex was astounded.

'Of course she is.' Marly was hard put to it to keep a straight face. 'But it's the custom for a wife to retain her family name and just add the word Khun, to show she has a husband. It's a little more complicated than that, but I don't wish to confuse you.'

'Thank God for that! You've already confused me enough!'

She laughed, and taking it as a sign that she might be weakening, he repeated his request that she have dinner with him.

'I'm expected at home,' she reiterated.

'Can't you call them and say your boss has asked you to work late and then have dinner with him?'

'I couldn't show such disrespect to Nan's parents.' Marly came as close as she dared to showing offence. 'Not when they treat me as if I were their daughter.'

'Why is it disrespectful? You're single, and free to have dinner with me or anyone else you like.'

'But tonight I am not free. I have given a promise and it would offend my elders if I changed my plans.'

Alex muttered under his breath, and Marly eyed him soulfully.

'The other evening you said you preferred docile women,' she reminded him in the gentlest of voices. 'But I see now that you mean docile to *your* wishes.'

He got the point instantly and his eyebrows rose in surprise. 'You see me as autocratic, then?'

'It is not seemly for me to comment on your character.'

'You just have—by implication!'

'I'm sorry.' Marly fluttered her hands at him and tried to look distressed. 'I didn't mean to offend you. I was merely illustrating the inconsistency of your attitude.'

'Very successfully too,' he said wryly. 'I'll watch my step in future.'

'You aren't angry with me?'

'Definitely not.'

To prove it, he set out to charm her, and she had to keep all her wits about her not to be bowled over. How difficult it was to believe he was nothing more than a two-timing wolf in sheep's clothing!

'Let's finish this before I take you home,' he said, lifting up the quarter-full bottle of champagne.

Shaking her head, Marly rose to leave, and without demur he followed. He had learned his lesson well, she thought, hiding a smile.

Only as his car drew to a stop outside her friend's house did she wonder whether she had taken her act too far in refusing to spend the evening with him. Nan would have had no hesitation in asking her parents to excuse her from dinner. Except Marly knew that had she fallen in with his plans too easily he might have equated her with the other girls he knew—none of whom, she was sure, would have dreamed of refusing an invitation to go out with him.

Glancing at his beautifully etched profile, she noticed that his lids were lowered in a frown. Was it with disappointment or frustration? Perhaps if he became too frustrated by her behaviour he might decide to look elsewhere for his pleasure, which was not what she wanted. She took a deep breath and spoke.

'Would you care to join us for dinner?'

Startled, he swung round in his seat to stare at her. 'I don't want to impose.'

'You wouldn't be. The professor keeps open house and you will be most welcome.'

'Then I'd be delighted to accept.'

Though Marly was nervous of having Alex see her in Nan's house for any length of time—afraid that one or other of the family might inadvertently give her away— any misgivings she had were instantly dispelled by Nan's wink as she walked in with him.

Within a few moments Alex was sitting cross-legged next to the professor, on a woven cushion on the floor; whiskies in hand, they were deep in conversation, discussing the problems of the world. She stifled a giggle at the way Alex was trying to fold his long legs in front of him and tuck his feet out of sight—as everyone in the room was doing as a matter of course, for Thais considered it bad manners to point their feet towards you.

'Mr Hamilton doesn't seem able to get comfortable,' commented Nan's mother, going over to him. 'Would you be happier sitting on a chair, Mr Hamilton?'

'Thank you, but I'm fine as I am,' he lied with a smile.

Khun Ladda was too diplomatic to persist further, and inclining her head, went back to her cushion.

'I can see why Andrea fell for him,' Nan whispered to Marly. 'He's so sexy I could go for him myself.'

'In a little while he won't find it so easy to be charming,' Marly said, an imp of mischief sparkling her eyes. 'I didn't invite him to dinner because I wanted his company.'

'What are you up to?'

'Wait and see.'

Quietly she left the room and crossed the courtyard to the sturdily built hut that served as the kitchen, thus keeping the main house free from cooking smells. The only similarity to a Western-style kitchen was the refrigerator, for there was no oven, microwave, or any other labour-saving gadget. All fruit and vegetables were cut and chopped by hand-held knives, and all food cooked on the double gas hob that dominated one wall, or grilled on the charcoal brazier that dominated another. Yet the variety of recipes was so astonishing that the lack of roasts, or cakes and biscuits, was not missed.

Aroon, the family cook, who rose at dawn each day to go to market to buy all the fresh food, was busy stir-frying at the gas hob, and a delicious smell of garlic, ginger and lime filled the air.

'What's for dinner tonight, Aroon?' she asked in Thai, peering into the three woks—high-rimmed, round-bottomed frying-pans that were the only cooking pots he used.

He rattled off the names of three dishes and she nodded appreciatively. Two of them—lemon shrimp soup and fish cakes—were her special favourites, the soup being flavoured with coconut milk and lime, the fish cakes with coriander leaves and spring onions. It was the third dish—red curry beef—that made her eye the cook warily, and he grinned back at her.

'I know you don't enjoy it too spicy,' he said, 'so I'll take out a portion for you before I add the chillies. You want me to do the same for the guest?'

'That won't be necessary. He likes it very hot.'

'As hot as the family do?' Aroon asked in amazement.

'Oh, yes. The hotter the better,' Marly said with a mischievous smile, then, wiping it from her face, returned to the living-room.

'Well?' Nan whispered as Marly joined her. 'Will you let me in on the secret now?'

'I've been telling Aroon that Alex adores hot food, so he needn't go easy on the chillies.'

'Is that true?'

'I shouldn't think so for a minute. When I had dinner with him at the Shangri-la, he picked out every chilli he could see and put them on another plate!'

'My God! Aroon's curry will burn him to a frazzle!'

'That's the intention,' Marly said gleefully. 'And *you*, dear Nan, have to distract Alex when the food arrives, so that he doesn't notice that Aroon's prepared a separate bowl for me. I want him to think I'm eating the same meal he is.'

Shortly afterwards, a maid wheeled in a trolley laden with fragrant dishes of food and set them out on the large, low table in the centre of the living-room.

'I'm delighted you've given me the chance of dining in a private home,' Alex murmured, coming to stand beside Marly as they all crowded round the table. 'It looks so marvellous I don't know where to begin.'

'You can have lemon shrimp soup as a starter, or sip it during your meal, as *we* do,' she said, sinking gracefully on to a cushion.

'I may as well do it Thai style while I'm about it,' he replied, lowering himself on to the floor beside her and folding his long legs in front of him, yoga fashion. 'I suppose one does eventually get used to sitting like this?' he enquired.

'In a year or two!'

He laughed, then nodded towards the bowl of steaming beef in its red sauce. 'That looks interesting. What is it?'

'Red curry beef—a great favourite with all the family. You should eat it with rice.'

Nan, who had followed Marly's instructions and was sitting on the other side of him, touched his forearm. 'It's an honour having you here with us, Mr Hamilton.'

'The honour is mine. It's extremely kind of your family to make me so welcome.'

As Nan played her part and kept his attention, Marly filled her own plate from the smaller bowl of red beef curry that Aroon had prepared for her, then signalled for a maid to take the bowl away.

'Will you help me to this dish you recommend so highly?' Alex said, turning back to Marly.

Gracefully she reached for a plate, heaped a mound of rice on it, and topped it with the steaming beef and a goodly portion of its dark red sauce. Smiling sweetly at him, she lifted a spoonful of her own portion to her mouth and ate it.

'If it tastes as good as your expression,' he commented, 'I'll be coming back for a second helping.'

Only when pigs can fly! she thought, and from beneath her lashes watched him put a forkful into his mouth and start chewing. Almost at once his tanned skin took on a deeper hue as a hot tide of colour swept into his face. Beads of perspiration erupted on his forehead and upper lip, and he frantically waved one hand in front of his gasping mouth and reached for his water glass with the other.

'Did something go down the wrong way?' she questioned innocently.

He tried to speak but couldn't, and she hastily poured him another glass of water, which he downed at a gulp.

'My God,' he gasped finally, his normally deep voice thin and strangled. 'That has to be the hottest curry in the world! I thought my mouth had caught fire!'

'I'm terribly sorry, Alex. I should have warned you about the chillies.'

'I'm surprised you didn't,' Nan's mother interposed. 'Mr Hamilton could have shared——' She stopped as she read the warning expression in Marly's eyes, and her own registered surprise that Marly could play such a cruel joke on him. Lifting another plate from the pile on the table, she handed it to him. 'Try some *sa-koo piak*, Mr Hamilton.'

'Not for the moment, thanks.' Taking another sip of water, he mopped his brow with a crisp white handkerchief.

'Do change your mind. It will relieve the burning in your throat.'

'It will?'

'I promise you. It's similar to an English sago pudding, though here we add mauve yam roots and shredded coconut.'

Putting a ladleful on his plate, he tentatively spooned some into his mouth. 'Mmm, you're right, it does ease the burning.'

Quickly he swallowed some more, and Marly, watching him, saw there was still a faint film of perspiration on his skin. He had really gone through fire tonight to be with her! Yet though she was ashamed of the trick she had played on him, she did not regret it. Why should she, when he had played a far worse trick on Andrea?

Yet later that evening, walking through the courtyard with him to his car, she again acted contrite. After all, it was the polite thing to do if you had nearly burned your guest to death!

'I'm really sorry about the chillies, Alex,' she apologised again. 'I'm so used to them that I forgot how hot they can be to a Western palate.'

'I wish you'd stop regarding me as a Westerner,' he muttered, placing his hands round her waist, 'and simply see me as a man. A man who can't think of anything else except you, who wants you to feel the same way towards *him*.'

If only that were feasible, Marly thought on a sigh, knowing that Alex would always be equated in her mind with Andrea.

'Do you believe that's possible?' he went on, drawing her so close that the beat of his heart came through the soft cambric of his shirt and the silk of her bodice.

Taking a shaky breath, she wondered how long she could maintain indifference to the strength of the long, lean body pressed so close to hers. Thank heaven she had not agreed to have dinner alone with him! This way there was no chance of his giving her more than a good-night kiss. Had they been alone, she might have been in danger of falling victim to his potent sexuality.

Wrenching free of him, she stepped back into the compound and closed the gate. 'Sweet dreams, Alex,' she said, glad she was acting Thai and could lower her eyes and avoid his smouldering ones. 'I'll see you in the office tomorrow.'

'You haven't answered my question.'

'I know.'

'I won't always be satisfied with silence.'

'I know that too.'

Before he could reply, she glided into the dark shadow of a jacaranda tree, remaining motionless so that he could no longer see her.

'You're a tantalising witch, my beautiful Marly,' he whispered through the gate. 'And you're weaving a potent spell around me. But I'm a pretty good weaver myself, so watch out!'

It was a warning Marly had every intention of taking to heart.

CHAPTER SEVEN

MARLY had a restless night, her sleep disturbed by vivid dreams of Alex making love to her and, what was even more disturbing, of her wild response to him!

As dawn turned the sky from midnight-blue to pink to gold, heralding yet another perfect day, she plumped up her pillows and let her thoughts wander at will. Naturally they turned to her dreams, and with the honesty that was a part of her character—at least until she had embarked on this masquerade—she admitted she was half in love with him. Indeed from the moment she had seen him he had struck a chord in her that should have served as a warning. Trouble was, she had been so set on avenging Andrea she had given no thought to the emotional pit opening up in front of herself. And now she had fallen into it!

She sighed heavily. No longer could she feign indifference to the way Alex looked at her, spoke to her, touched her. Damn it, he seemed so sincere and caring, it was difficult to believe he had asked Andrea to be his wife simply to get her into his bed. In fact it didn't make sense. With his sexual magnetism he probably had more trouble keeping women *out* of his bed!

When Andrea had told her the whole unhappy saga, she had accepted it at face value, but since coming to know Alex she found it difficult to envisage him as the unscrupulous swine she had first thought him to be. What if he had genuinely believed he loved Andrea and then discovered—once they were living together—that they were not as compatible as he had thought?

Andrea was a delightful person, but even her best friends, indeed especially her best friends, had to admit she could be maddeningly scatter-brained when the mood took her; and Alex—whom Marly had found to be a logical and methodical man—might well have been driven to distraction by it. Therefore, if it had caused him to have second thoughts about marriage, wasn't it better to have said so before the ceremony rather than after it?

'Ten bahts for your thoughts,' someone offered, and with a start Marly saw Nan at the foot of her bed.

'They aren't worth it,' she shrugged.

'From the look on your face I'd say they were worth more. What's bothering you?' Nan perched on the side of her bed. 'Or should I say who?'

'Draw in your line,' Marly replied, stifling a yawn.

'Come again?'

'Stop fishing.'

'I think you're in love with Alex,' Nan stated, never one to beat about the bush.

'Don't be ridiculous. If he were the last man on earth——'

'I'd fight you for him!'

'It wouldn't be necessary; I'd give him to you. He's not my type. He's too smooth, too sure of himself, too——'

'"The lady doth protest too much, methinks"!' Nan quoted deadpan.

'And *me* thinks you're way off-beam!'

'No, I'm not. I've known you a long time, remember, and the vibes you give off when Alex is with you...'

'OK, so I fancy him,' Marly capitulated. 'But it's no more than that.'

'I hope not. A man who does the dirty on one woman can do it on another.'

'What if he genuinely loved Andrea and suddenly found he had changed his mind?'

Nan considered this for a moment, then shook her head. 'Alex Hamilton is the sort of man who reasons things out before making any decision. He isn't the sort to think something one day and change his mind the next.'

'It wasn't the next day, Nan. He lived with Andrea for six weeks; long enough to realise he'd made a mistake. I mean, why should we assume the worst of him? Why not give him the benefit of the doubt?'

'Because Andrea is a friend of ours, that's why!'

'Perhaps we've been prejudiced in her favour because of it,' Marly replied. 'I love her dearly but she isn't without faults. None of us is.'

'True,' Nan agreed. 'I guess you have a point. So what will you do? Tell Alex who you really are?'

'Yes. I won't say why I embarked on the act, though. I'll let him think it was because he originally mistook me for Thai, and I carried on the game for a joke.'

'Will you tell him you're a friend of Andrea's?'

'Yes. That will give him a chance to tell me *his* side of the story.' Marly nibbled at her lip. 'I wonder if he'll fancy me when he learns I'm not Miss Docile but a liberated lady who believes in equality?'

'I don't see why he shouldn't,' Nan placated. 'Meet me for lunch and tell me how things went.'

'I won't do it during office hours. I'll wait till he takes me out and is nice and relaxed.'

Glad that her charade would soon be at an end, Marly dressed to go to work. Although it was Saturday, both she and Alex were due at the office to finish off some work from yesterday. She would have liked to wear her hair centre-parted and straight to her shoulders, but she knew that twisting it into a chignon in the style worn by Queen Sikrit gave her an air of calm and maturity, and she required both these attributes until she had come clean with Alex.

No sooner had she entered her office than he strode in, and the way her heart leapt in her throat told her how foolish she was to have thought she hadn't yet fallen for him too hard. If she fell any harder, she'd make a hole in the floor! In a beige linen suit he resembled the proverbial golden Apollo, from his tawny mane of hair brushed back from his forehead to the glow of his skin. Only his eyes weren't golden. But then they weren't grey either this morning, but held a dark flame whose heat made her painfully aware of her susceptibility to him.

The urge to confess the truth was so strong that she knew she had to tell him now. Only then could she admit she was a friend of Andrea's, and ask to hear his version of why he had changed his mind about marrying her.

'Alex, I——'

'I'm leaving for Hong Kong in an hour,' he spoke at the same time, then stopped and smiled. 'Sorry, I seem to have cut across you. You were saying?'

No way could she make her confession now. 'It can wait till you return,' she parried. 'How long will you be gone?'

'I'm not sure. A few days at least.'

'Business or pleasure?' she asked composedly.

'Pleasure—if you come with me.'

Her hands fluttered in mock horror. 'Oh, no, I couldn't do that.'

'I promise to behave honourably.'

'The answer is still no.'

'Pity.' His level regard held wry humour. 'It would have been enjoyable—and could have been memorable.' Reaching out, he placed his hands on her shoulders and drew her close. The dark flame in the grey eyes ranged over her, and his lower lip moved sensuously, as if it were already tasting her. 'May I?' he asked, his face coming inexorably closer.

Not waiting for an answer, he brought his mouth down on hers. Expecting passion and demand, she was surprised by gentleness and restraint, and was debating whether to part her lips to him when he lifted his head from hers and stepped back.

'I don't think there's any need for me to say be good,' he murmured, 'so I'll just say think of me.'

With a lift of a long-fingered, tanned hand, he was gone, and Marly sank on to her chair, wondering why he had so easily accepted her refusal to go with him to Hong Kong. Had he really desired her company, or had the invitation merely been a reflex action; one he automatically meted out to any attractive girl he met? It was not a pleasant thought but it could not be discounted.

The telephone rang and she hurriedly lifted it.

'I tried you at home,' Kevin said. 'How come you're working on a Saturday?'

'I'm finishing off something.'

'Can you finish it off later and come for a swim? I'll meet you at the pool after my squash game. I'll be an hour.'

'Lovely idea,' she said. An hour was ample to complete the notes she had to do, and leave them on Alex's desk ready for his return.

She still had fifteen minutes to spare when she went next door to his office. The whole suite was deserted, his secretary having taken the morning off, and she found it strange to be so aware of his presence despite his not being there. She was standing in the centre of the room, the smell of his aftershave in her nostrils—though this might have been imagination—when the door opened and a light, feminine voice said, 'Alex, darling! I went up to your apartment but you weren't...'

The words trailed off as the two women looked at one another. We sure are a contrast, Marly thought, gazing at the tall, slender blonde whose pale blue eyes were regarding her with open frankness.

'Are you Alex's secretary?'

'No. She's not here this morning. I'm doing the software programing for the hotel.' Marly introduced herself, remembering to give the Thai version of her name.

'Alex mentioned he was having a special software program installed, but I didn't realise it was being devised by a woman.' Colour stained the pale skin. 'Oh, dear, that sounds rude, and I——'

'I understand, Miss——?'

'Fiona Danziger. I'm going to marry Alex.' Soft pink lips curved in a smile. 'When I can find him, that is!'

Marly felt as though she had been hit in the stomach. So much for her belief that she had misjudged him! Everything Andrea had said about him was true—except that he was a bigger swine than she had first imagined!

'You're—you're going to marry him?' she echoed when she could speak. She knew the question was stupid—hadn't the girl already said so?—but she still had the urge to get confirmation.

'When he stops running!' came the reply. 'Where is he?'

'He left for Hong Kong this morning.'

'What a bore! I wish now that I'd told him I was coming here, but I wanted it to be a surprise.'

It certainly will be, Marly thought, and couldn't wait to hear how Alex would explain away his fiancée to her. Or maybe he wouldn't bother. After all, he had been pretty laconic when he had left Andrea, and might not feel that Marly—whom he had simply been dating—even warranted an explanation.

'I can see you're astonished,' Fiona Danziger went on. 'I suppose the poor darling's been dating every glamour-puss in Bangkok?'

'Poor darling?' Marly repeated unbelievingly. 'Don't you mind?'

'How can I? He has no choice. Our fair sex throw themselves at him like lemmings off a cliff! Trouble is, he's too kind-hearted to turn them down. That's why I think it's best if we got married, though he's still worried that I'm too young and may regret it later.'

She perched on the edge of an armchair, one long, shapely leg swinging idly. She was no more than twenty, and had an untouched air that was genuine. Never in a million years would Marly have considered her Alex's type, yet now that she knew she was, she could suddenly see why, for an ingenuous female was more likely to remain unaware of his womanising. Indeed, married to Fiona, he wouldn't have to change his lifestyle one iota!

'I realise I don't look Alex's type,' the soft young voice continued artlessly, 'but that's my strength, don't you think?'

'I—er——'

'I've known Alex since I was nine and he was twenty-three. Our mothers were best friends, and when my parents were killed in a road accident, his family adopted me. I was ready to marry him when I was eighteen, but Alex felt I should see more of the world first, meet other men...'

'And did you?' Marly couldn't help asking.

'Masses. But none could hold a candle to him. That's why I'm here—to tell him I'll never love anyone else, and to set our wedding date. Once we have, I'll fly home and put the arrangements in hand. Do you have any idea when he'll be back?'

'I'm not quite sure. A few days, I think.'

'That's not too bad. If it were longer, I'd join him.'
The girl stood up. 'I think I'll unpack and go down for
a swim. See you later.'

'Miss Danziger?'

The girl swung round. 'Yes?'

Marly moistened lips that had suddenly grown dry.
She longed to tell Fiona exactly the sort of man her future
husband was, yet staring into the guileless face she
realised she would be wasting her time.

'I—er—just wondered if I could get you anything?'
she mumbled.

'No, thanks. The Hamilton hotels are home away from
home for me, and I have everything I want.'

Including the son and heir, Marly thought bitterly
when Fiona had gone, and sank on to the nearest chair.
The perfidy of the man! He obviously intended marrying
Fiona at some stage, but meanwhile was not letting it
cramp his love-life. She could almost pity the girl for
the marriage she would have, for no way could she see
him as faithful.

Yet why feel superior to Fiona when she had been
equally naïve—and with far less reason, for Andrea had
warned her the sort of man he was? Yet one glance into
his smoky grey irises and she had fallen under his spell
like a lovesick schoolgirl. Remembering that an hour ago
she had argued with Nan in his favour, she was filled
with shame. It permeated every cell of her being and she
writhed with the agony of it.

'No!' she cried suddenly, jumping to her feet. 'I won't
let him get away with it. He was definitely falling for
me, and that makes him vulnerable.'

She relished the knowledge, determined that as soon
as Fiona returned to England she would use his vulner-
ability to pay him back for the heartache he had caused.
Thank goodness she had not had a chance to confess
her charade to him.

Returning to her office, she locked her desk, picked up her bag and headed for the lift. Punching the button, and wishing it were Alex's well shaped nose, she stepped inside and went down to the lower ground floor and the hotel shopping centre to buy a swimsuit and cotton robe. But even as she riffled through the excellent selection, she was filled with disgust for him. The emotion disturbed her, for she was afraid it might destroy her judgement, and when it came to dealing with this two-timing Lothario, she needed all the judgement she possessed.

As usual, the lush green lawns abutting the vast swimming-pool were dotted with sunbeds, the majority shaded by palms. Those that were ranged around the pool itself were shaded by pink and yellow umbrellas, giving the scene a festive air that in no way matched her mood, which was grey, bordering on black!

But it was difficult to remain despondent when surrounded by holiday-makers all intent on having a good time, though she was glad that for the most part they did it quietly, due in no small measure to the staff, whose duty it was to see that transistors were played low and children kept under control. Not that there were many children present, for they had their own pool on the lower terrace.

She had already had a swim and was lounging on a sunbed when Kevin appeared, skin flushed, hair tousled and damp from the shower after his squash game. A thin terry robe was loosely belted round his waist, and as he dropped it down on the sunbed next to her, she saw he was more ruggedly built than he appeared when fully dressed. It made her wonder whether Alex would be the opposite. Muscular and magnificent in clothes, was he puny and pale in the nude? Who was she kidding? He'd be sensational.

'I'm glad you could see me,' Kevin said, sitting down with a contented sigh. 'There's nothing like a beautiful woman for giving meaning to a beautiful day.'

'I bet you have a beautiful bedside manner too!' Marly forced a smile to her lips, not wishing to spoil Kevin's mood.

'I try my best, and with you it requires no effort.' He slid her a quizzical glance. 'What's eating you? When I spoke to you an hour ago, you were happy as a sandboy. Is it anything to do with boss man?'

'Unfortunately, yes.' Careful not to disclose her personal hurt, Marly told him about Fiona, and had the pleasure of seeing his jaw drop incredulously.

'It's hard to believe the guy is such a louse!' he exclaimed. 'It puts his behaviour to your friend Andrea in a worse light than you thought.'

Marly nodded. 'And look how strongly he's been coming on to me. He had the nerve to invite me to go with him to Hong Kong!'

'What do you intend doing now that his fiancée is on the scene?'

'She won't be staying long, and once she's gone I'm sure he'll pretend he's going to break with her, and I'll pretend to believe him.'

'Be careful you don't get your fingers burnt.'

'What's that supposed to mean?' Marly asked, knowing full well that, like Nan, he was warning her not to lose her heart to Alex.

As Kevin went to reply, his mouth dropped open and his eyes glazed over.

Curious to know why he was looking pole-axed, Marly glanced round and saw Fiona sauntering along the path. She was dressed in a hyacinth-blue bikini that showed off her creamy skin and other more voluptuous attributes, and Kevin's eyes weren't the only male ones to follow her.

'That's Alex's fiancée,' Marly muttered as Fiona, passing by on her way to secure a lounging chair, saw her and hesitated.

Before she could move on, Kevin jumped to his feet and extended his hand, leaving Marly no option but to introduce him. Before she knew what was happening, he had settled Fiona in a chair beside them and ordered fresh pineapple juice all round.

'All I need is Alex here and it would be perfect.' Fiona sipped her drink and stretched out her long, shapely legs on the foot-rest.

'Alex?' Kevin asked, playing dumb.

'Alex Hamilton, my future husband.'

In her soft, breathless manner, she repeated the story she had told Marly, and Kevin listened as though hearing it for the first time.

'You need a swim to cheer you up,' he suggested when she came to the end. 'I'm sure your fiancé wouldn't want you to be miserable while you're waiting for him to return.'

As he finished speaking, Fiona gracefully rose and padded across to the shimmering water. 'Race you to the end!' she cried, and dived in, Kevin hard on her heels.

He beat her by a yard, but Marly recognised she was an excellent swimmer. She was probably good at all sport, just the kind of woman Alex would go for. Well, she herself was no mean sportswoman either, though her lack of inches and delicate build was against her when it came to tennis or squash.

She watched the two of them cavorting together, splashing, laughing, and throwing water over each other. The girl's fly-away blonde hair lay wet and limp on her shoulders, and liquid droplets sparkled on her thick-fringed lashes. Unlike most other women who, when soaked, looked their worst, Fiona was more stunning than ever, for it served to emphasise the naturalness of her beauty: glowing skin, baby-blue eyes sparkling, perfectly proportioned body vibrant with vitality.

Quickly Marly lay back and shut her eyes to the scene, but instead the tableau changed to Fiona and Alex, his dark head bent to her blonde one, their naked bodies entwined. Jealousy, sharp as a dagger, brought her upright, and she saw Kevin and Fiona somersaulting together in the water—a far more suitable couple, she decided!

CHAPTER EIGHT

MARLY managed to avoid seeing Fiona in the next few days, for, bumping into her in the corridor on her way to her office the morning after their swim, she had stopped her from coming in for a chat by the simple expedient of saying she had to complete her software program for the hotel by a specific date, and was already behind schedule.

But her main reason was that the girl irritated her with her constant references to Alex, and how much they loved each other. Not that Marly gave a damn! Far from it. It was simply that she found the subject boring—the subject of their love, of course, not the man himself. That would be impossible!

Three days later he walked into her office. Marly, engrossed in her work, did not hear him come in, and only when a shadow fell across her desk and computer screen did she glance round.

'Alex!'

She jumped up and backed away from him, then stopped, angry with herself for the confusion she displayed. But then it was normal to be confused when one's boss walked in unexpectedly, looking like every woman's dream in a tropical-weight cream suit that heightened the bronze of his skin and threw his silver-grey eyes into relief.

'Why are you startled?' he smiled.

'You're back sooner than I thought.'

'I missed you too much to stay away longer.'

Unfortunately it was a sentiment she endorsed, but she was not going to admit it. If truth be told, she was furious to find she still had any feelings for him whatsoever.

'I have a surprise for you,' she said quietly.

'You have?' He spoke softly too, his expression telling her he was only half listening, his eyes too busy devouring her.

Marly was wearing her butterfly-wing cheong-sam, and with her hair sculptured away from her face she could have stepped straight from Puccini's opera. But there all resemblance to Madam Butterfly ended, for she was no innocent girl taken in by a callous lover, but a liberated lady intent on bringing a womaniser to heel.

'What kind of surprise?' he went on.

'Your fiancée is here.'

'My *who*?'

What a marvellous actor he was! His confusion appeared completely genuine.

'Miss Danziger,' Marly stated.

'Fiona? I don't believe it!'

'You should.'

'When did she get here?' he grated.

'The day you left for Hong Kong. She came—and I quote—to inform you she's ready to set the date for your wedding.'

Alex's mouth thinned to a grim line, and his eyes darkened to deep, smoky grey. Little wonder he was taking the news badly; so would any Casanova on learning his fiancée had arrived to clip his wings.

'I'd better go and talk to her,' he said curtly. 'I'll see you later.'

Alone again, Marly returned to her computer. Alex had looked less than delighted to learn of Fiona's arrival, and she could not help feeling sympathy for her. Yet surely the girl must have known that someone as charismatic as Alex Hamilton wasn't going to spend his nights going to bed with a book! But obviously Fiona trusted him, just as Andrea had, and probably all the other women in his complicated life.

With an effort Marly tried to concentrate on the software she was creating, but the letters were a jumble and she finally turned her back on the screen. How would Alex explain away Fiona? If he had been here when she arrived, he might have tried to keep her identity secret, but now his only option was to brazen it out. And knowing him, brazen it out he would!

Bitterness swamped her as she admitted he had only been amusing himself with her, and her belief that he might have genuinely fallen in love with her was just an illusion. Like the cuckoo he would go his selfish way, stealing and plundering whatever took his fancy, with no regard for the pain and damage he left behind him.

Glancing at her watch, she saw it was time to go home. Switching off her computer and slinging her bag over her shoulder, she was at the door when the telephone rang. Automatically she reached for it, tensing as she heard Alex's secretary say he wished to see her in his office.

'It's past six and I'm leaving—I have another appointment,' Marly protested, deciding she'd had enough of acquiescing to his lordship's beck and call.

'Mr Hamilton sounded very—er—positive,' the woman stated, 'positive', as Marly very well knew, being a euphemism for brooking no argument.

'Very well, I'll be with him right away,' she answered, and knew from his secretary's expression as she walked into the outer office a few moments later that she had made the correct decision.

This was confirmed when she stood facing Alex across his desk, for he looked distinctly bad-tempered.

'You wanted to see me, Mr Hamilton?'

'Yes. We have things to talk over. Personal things.'

Ostentatiously she glanced at her watch, and the tightening of his mouth told her he hadn't missed the gesture.

'I realise it's after office hours,' he drawled, 'but that's the best time to discuss the personal, don't you think?'

Remembering her role, she lowered her head. 'I can't imagine what you have to say to me that's personal.'

'Give you the date of my wedding perhaps? How would you feel about that?'

Marly's heart missed a beat, then raced alarmingly. 'I'd be very happy for you.'

'Indeed?' He rose and came round the side of his desk, stopping so close to her that she was enveloped by the musky scent of him. 'If you told me *you* were going to be married, I'd be devastated.'

'I'd never leave without completing my contract,' she said swiftly, deliberately misunderstanding him.

'I don't give a damn for your contract, and you know it! Be honest with me. When you learned who Fiona was, weren't you even a little upset to think I'd taken you out and not mentioned I had a fiancée?'

Marly's slender shoulders rose in a shrug, allowing him to think what he liked.

'Except it isn't true,' he continued. 'I am not and never have been engaged to her.'

A billowing wave of joy surged through Marly, leaving no room for any other emotion. She forgot his callous treatment of her friend, forgot his reputation as a Lothario, forgot everything except the bliss of hearing what he had just told her. Yet as swiftly as logic left her, it returned, and so did her common sense.

'If what you say is true, why does Fiona carry on like this?'

'Because she believes that if she says it often enough, it will happen.'

Marly found this hard to accept. Admittedly the girl had struck her as naïve, but she wasn't stupid.

'I'm speaking the truth,' Alex reiterated, correctly reading the emotions chasing themselves across the face in front of him, and taking her hands in his warm, strong ones, lowered his lips to them.

Her heart turned over at sight of the thick, fringed lashes forming shadows on his cheekbones, and the way a tawny lock of hair fell forward on his forehead. She longed to accept what he had said, but was still scared of being duped by his sexual magnetism.

'Fiona's had a crush on me since she was a child,' he explained, and went on to repeat what the girl had told her about his parents taking her into their home when hers had died. 'To me, she was like a younger sister, and I treated her as such.'

'Not in *her* mind.'

'Lord knows why,' he said heavily. 'I've told her often enough. Trouble is we all spoiled her when she first came to live with us, and it became a habit. Perhaps if I'd been tougher with her when she started to hero-worship me, I might have scotched it on the head, but she was so gentle and vulnerable—like you in a way—that I found it impossible to hurt her. I just hoped my being away from home for most of the past three years would give her a chance to fall for someone else, but it doesn't seem she has.'

'Your charm is obviously too strong to be forgotten,' Marly said, still unsure whether Alex was being totally truthful. Were it not for his past behaviour she might have given him the benefit of the doubt, but as it was... 'You probably led her on without realising it,' she added.

'Definitely not.' Alex was incisive. 'I've played the field in my time—I won't deny it—but it's always with women who know the score, not young girls in the first flush of love. And one thing I've never done is mess with people's emotions.'

Oh, no? Marly longed to throw his words back in his face. What about Andrea? she cried silently. Don't you think *that* was messing with a person's emotions? With an enormous effort she said nothing, but all her previous antagonism towards him flared anew, determining her to carry on with her original plan. She could hardly wait for the day of reckoning when she could discard him as easily as he had discarded her friend.

'So how have you finally made Fiona accept the truth?' she forced herself to ask.

'I haven't.'

'*Haven't*?'

'I haven't yet told her.'

'You mean you're going to let her set a wedding date?'

'No matter what date she sets, I've no intention of marrying her.'

'Why can't you tell her so and clear the air?'

Alex's hesitation was palpable, then he sighed, as if coming to some conclusion. 'When Fiona came to live with us she never mentioned her parents or the accident that had killed them. The doctors said she had blocked out the entire event, and advised us not to refer to it until *she* did.'

'Which was when?'

'Years later, on her fifteenth birthday. She suddenly started talking of it and didn't stop—*couldn't* stop. It was painful to listen to her. She was like a person possessed. Eventually she had to go into a nursing home; it was a complete breakdown. It was afterwards, when she recovered and returned home, that she developed a crush on me. I tried to tease her out of it and hoped it would die the death as she grew older, but...' The broad shoulders lifted. 'And now she pitches up here with this incredible story of hers. In the normal course of events

I'd be blunt and brutal, but given her history I have to be careful.'

Marly found it in her heart to pity Fiona who, in the midst of finally facing up to the agonising loss of her parents, had seen in Alex a strong, stalwart lover to protect and cherish her forever.

'You have a problem on your hands,' she observed.

'But I think I've found a way of dealing with it. No matter what she says or does, I'll behave like a brother to her. I'll show her around but I won't take her out alone, only in a foursome—with you as one of the four!' For the first time since he had learned of the girl's arrival, Alex smiled. 'All we have to do is find some amiable young man who'll agree to make a play for her.'

'I can't see her playing back!'

'It's worth a try. Anyway, it will give *us* a chance of being together.'

Marly had to give him full marks for scheming. He could keep Fiona happy and chat up his next conquest at the same time. Talk about killing two birds with one stone! Yet his suggestion suited her perfectly, for the more Alex saw of her, the quicker he would fall for her.

'I don't think you'll have trouble finding a man for Fiona,' she said aloud. 'She a beautiful girl.'

'But you are beautiful and intelligent,' came the swift reply as a long finger traced the curving bow of Marly's upper lip. 'I've a friend at the British embassy who may be willing to help me.'

'Why don't I ask Kevin?' Marly suggested, deciding it would be nice to have him on hand, since he knew the act she was putting on and could be an ally. Alex looked distinctly put out, and seeing it as jealousy, she fanned the green-eyed monster. 'He'd be ideal. He's good-looking and fun to be with, yet he has a serious side too. I like him very much.'

'Really?' It was a clipped sound.

'And Fiona likes him too. She met him the day she arrived, when he was with me at the pool.'

'I'd prefer someone else.'

Marly fluttered her lashes and gave a tinkling little laugh. 'You can't be jealous of him!'

'I'm jealous of any man you know.'

'You flatter me.'

'Because I find you the loveliest girl I've ever met?'

'I'm sure you've known others far lovelier.'

'None who makes me feel as you do. And as an extra bonus, you don't act as if you want to rival me!'

'Don't bank on it,' she teased. 'I may yet decide to go into the hotel business! Many of our women hold down important jobs, you know.'

'But they manage to stay sweet and lovely with it,' he rejoined, 'and don't make their men feel insecure.'

'I can't imagine *you* being insecure.'

'I'm not.' Alex lounged back against his desk, and though his stance was indolent, power and determination flowed from him. 'But I know a number of men who feel as if they've been emasculated.'

Which is how you'll feel when I've finished with you, Marly thought, envisaging his shock when he discovered that a woman had made a fool of *him*, instead of the other way around.

'I still think Kevin is the right man to make up the foursome you want,' was what she said. 'Fiona met him through me, and won't be suspicious of him when he joins us.'

'You have a point there. So Kevin it is.'

'Shall I tell him the true position between you and Fiona?'

'Of course. If he thinks we're genuinely engaged he won't make a play for her—which is the whole purpose of the exercise.'

'She could get hurt.'

'Even more so if she continues throwing herself at *me*.'

How true! Marly thought. Any woman would suffer if she fell for Alex.

The intercom on his desk buzzed, and his secretary informed him there was a call from Hong Kong. Picking up the telephone, he signalled Marly to stay.

'Have dinner with Fiona and me,' he mouthed.

'I can't,' she whispered back, refusing to pander to him. He hadn't so much as rung her during his absence, and to return unannounced and expect her to be free for him was not on. 'I promised I'd be home to dinner.'

He looked as if he wanted to argue, but the voice at the other end of the line gave him no opportunity, and as he spoke into the receiver Marly took the opportunity of escaping.

It wasn't until that evening when dinner was over and she and Nan were alone together in her room that she was able to tell her of her conversation with Alex and what he had decided to do.

'He certainly has a devious mind,' Nan said. 'Do you think he's as innocent over Fiona as he maintains? With his record, he may well have given her encouragement.'

'I doubt it. She's a pretty girl but far too ingenuous to attract him.'

'The character *you're* pretending to be is ingenuous too.'

'But I'm doing it with subtlety!'

Nan blew her a raspberry, and before Marly could reply, Alex rang to speak to her.

'How far advanced are you with the software program?' he asked without preamble.

Uncertain where the question was going to lead her, she was careful with her answer. 'I'm ahead of schedule but problems can still occur. Why do you ask?'

'Because I wondered if you and Kevin would care to be my guests for a week in Phuket? A friend has offered

me the loan of his house there and I thought the four
of us could fly down the day after tomorrow.'

'It sounds very tempting,' Marly said, 'but I don't
know Kevin's schedule at the hospital.'

'Can you contact him and find out? I'll wait for your
call.'

'I'm too busy to do it now,' she lied, not wishing him
to think she was a puppet that jumped when he pulled
the string. 'I'll let you know some time tomorrow at the
office.'

'Don't accept the invitation,' Nan said as Marly replaced the telephone. 'Phuket's such a romantic island,
it will give Alex ideas.'

'He already has them!'

'All the more reason not to go there with him. I wish
you'd forget this charade of yours. Come clean with him
and tell him it was a joke you did for a bet.'

'And forget what he did to Andrea?'

'What good will it do her if you make him fall for
you and then laugh in his face?'

'You never said any of this when I first suggested the
idea.'

'Because I never thought you'd get emotionally in-
volved with him—and don't pretend you aren't. He isn't
capable of deep feelings, Marly, and he'll forget you long
before you forget him.' Nan's usual smiling face was
serious. 'I know you're halfway to being in love with
him, and I'd hate to see you hurt.'

'So you've already said. But you're worrying need-
lessly. He means nothing to me.' Marly gave her friend
a hug. 'Stop predicting doom and gloom and throw
yourself into the fun of it, like me. If turning the tables
on Alex does nothing other than clip the wings of one
chauvinistic predator, it will be worthwhile. Now if you'll
excuse me, I'll go telephone Kevin.'

As luck had it he was free for the weekend, as well as having several days' leave, but to her astonishment he was hesitant about making up a foursome.

'I thought you liked Fiona?' Marly quizzed.

'I do.'

'Then why the reluctance?'

'I don't go in for masochism. And the way she dotes on Alex Hamilton, no other guy stands a chance with her.'

'Except that she stands no chance with *him*.'

There was a momentary pause before Kevin spoke. 'You're kidding me.'

'No, I'm not.' As concisely as she could, Marly filled him in on the true story.

'Poor kid,' Kevin remarked when she had finished. 'Pity you can't tell her the way Alex let down your friend Andrea. It would put paid to her fantasies.'

'I doubt it. She'd probably find loads of reasons to explain away his behaviour.'

'If she's so besotted over him, what chance do I have with her?' Kevin demanded, his tone dry.

'You can be her shoulder to cry on when Alex leaves her alone and flirts with me; and you know the old adage about catching someone on the rebound?'

'Thanks a million. You do wonders for my ego!'

Marly bit her lip. 'If you don't want to come, I'll understand. Alex has a friend at the embassy who——'

'No, I'll do it.' Kevin was brusque. 'At least if it's me, I'll be gentle with her when I pick up the pieces. Let me know where and when to meet you, and I'll be there.'

Ending the call, Marly swung round to face Nan. 'It's all fixed.'

'Fixed being the operative word,' Nan said drily. 'I don't know who's the bigger schemer—you or Alex.'

'I'd say it's a photo finish!'

'At least promise me you'll end it when you get back from Phuket? If you can't have him grovelling at your feet by the end of a week in paradise island, you should give up!'

'I promise I will,' Marly asserted. 'And that day can't come quickly enough for me.'

CHAPTER NINE

MARLY did not see Alex till half an hour before their departure for Phuket, a rarely occurring migraine having laid her low for twenty-four hours.

Nan had spoken to him, however, explaining Marly's absence and saying she and Kevin would meet him at the airport, and she was not in the least surprised when he sent a limousine to collect them.

'Your boss does things in style,' Kevin remarked, leaning back against the soft leather seat of the Mercedes. 'But I guess that's easy when you're heir to the Hamilton chain. I suppose that's why women go for him?'

She gave a non-committal murmur, cognisant of the fact that Alex's style and appeal to women was not dependent on money. Even poor, he would exude style; it was part and parcel of him.

This realisation was brought home to her when she entered the VIP departure lounge and he rose from his chair and strolled leisurely towards them, relaxed into holiday mood in casual beige trousers and cream cotton top, the short sleeves disclosing bronzed arms with a fine sprinkling of dark hair. There were no accoutrements of wealth around him yet he conjured up an image of power and authority. That was what attracted women, she acknowledged; that, plus his good looks and potent virility.

'Are you fully recovered?' he enquired, nodding to Kevin and then giving her his whole attention.

'Yes, thanks. I'm fine.'

Before she could say any more, Fiona joined them, arrestingly dressed in a blue mini sundress that showed off her long, shapely legs to perfection, and was the same colour as her large ingenuous eyes. Not all that ingenuous if you studied them carefully, Marly noted, aware of a wilfulness in them that was echoed in the slight thrust of the chin, a wilfulness that Alex, blinded by affection, misread as vulnerable.

'I'm so pleased you were well enough to make it, Marly. Otherwise this silly man of mine was threatening to call off the trip.' A limpid blue gaze rested on him meltingly. 'He was worried in case I'd be bored alone with him.'

Linking her arm through Alex's, she stayed close to his side as they settled down to wait for their boarding call.

'Thanks for inviting me to Phuket,' Kevin said to his host. 'I spent a few days there not long after I arrived in Thailand, and I've always wanted to go back.'

'What stopped you?' Fiona asked. 'I'm sure you could have found a job in a hospital there.'

'I didn't come here just to find a job,' he smiled, 'but to study under Professor Damrong.'

'Don't you get tired of studying? When I was at school I couldn't wait to leave!'

Both men smiled indulgently, and Marly marvelled at the way males—no matter how intelligent—always enjoyed the company of a bimbo. As she thought it, Alex turned his head towards her and raised his eyes heavenwards, and she instantly and happily revised her opinion of one male at least!

'Where exactly are we staying?' she asked.

'At Karon Beach. My friend's home is built on the shore and you can practically go from bed to sea.'

'Sounds idyllic,' Kevin put in.

'The whole island's idyllic—and we can use Jack's boat to explore it, and all the nearby islands as well.' A tawny head swivelled in Marly's direction. 'I suppose you've been to Phuket often?'

'This is the first time. I've been too busy working.'

'I can't think of you as a career woman,' Fiona said prettily. 'In England they're all into power-dressing and competing with men.'

'Thai women are competitive too, though we take more pains to disguise it.'

'That's probably why I enjoy living here,' Alex teased. 'I don't feel the draught of competition!'

'You wouldn't feel it regardless of where you lived,' Fiona stated. 'You're invulnerable!'

'Would that I were.'

Marly's eyes turned to him. Leaning back in his chair, smiling and relaxed, he gave the lie to his comment. Fiona was right. He *was* invulnerable; so confident of his power that he could afford to be indulgent of rivalry. And that applied to his personal life too, for the gods had showered him with gifts. What did he know of unrequited love, of sleepless nights, days of depression, of tears shed and unshed? They were for the trail of broken hearts he left behind him, while he went happily on to pastures new. And for the moment she was the object of his desire. The attraction she felt for him washed over her with renewed force, making a mockery of her assertion to Nan that she was indifferent to him.

Hurriedly she focused on Kevin. Despite knowing he was a doctor—and a damn good one according to Professor Damrong—she couldn't help regarding him as a lightweight; yet how much happier her future would be if she had fallen for *him* instead of Alex.

'What's the night-life like?' Fiona suddenly demanded.

'There's more than enough discos to satisfy you,' Alex informed her with a lazy grin. 'I take it you're still crazy about dancing?'

The girl's nod and smile showed a set of small white teeth, and watching her catch his hand and hold it against the hollow between her breasts, Marly thought that here was another person on whom the gods had lavished many gifts. No wonder Kevin was bowled over. Could Alex have been bowled over too, and made promises he no longer wanted to keep, as had happened with Andrea?

With a feeling of relief she heard their flight called, and they gathered their hand luggage and boarded the plane.

Fiona sat at a window-seat for two, with Alex next to her, and Marly and Kevin took the two behind them. The noise of the engines prevented her from hearing their conversation, but she could not avoid the intimate gestures the girl lavished on him, her hand resting frequently on his arm, fluttering over his cheek or touching his leg. Kevin glowered, and for the first time since she had met him he was ill-humoured, giving away more of his feelings than he realised.

Determinedly Marly concentrated on the passing scene below her. Nan had spoken rapturously of the beauty of the islands to the south of Thailand, and it was plain she hadn't exaggerated, for with the sun still high in the summer sky Thai Airlines flew them low over one luxurious landscape after another. Not for nothing did the travel brochures dub this part of the country 'paradise'. Enraptured, she gazed at the string of beaches, bays, headlands and coves, and lushly covered mountains emerging from an azure sea.

But it was Phuket that was the ultimate jewel, and carefully descending the gangway in her flowered cheongsam, and breathing in the tangy sea air, she felt a sense of excitement.

'Strange you've never been here,' Alex remarked, walking alongside her.

'We vacation at another part of the coast,' she murmured, keeping her wits about her. 'It's nearer to
Bangkok, and just as lovely.' As she spoke, she prayed
he wouldn't ask her the name of it. The fat would really
be in the fire if he did. Hastily she fluttered her lashes
at him. 'But being here with you gives Phuket the
advantage.'

A tawny eyebrow lifted. 'That's the first compliment
you've paid me.'

'Alex!' Fiona called. 'Wait for me!'

Muttering under his breath, he stopped walking, and
Marly continued on her way alone until Kevin caught
up with her.

'She can't bear to let him out of her sight,' he grunted.
'Beats me what she sees in him. He's far too old for her.'

'I wouldn't exactly say he's ready for a bathchair!'

'I guess I'm jealous,' Kevin admitted sheepishly. 'But
he has everything going for him.'

'You're no slouch yourself,' Marly said kindly. 'And
I bet you're a killer at sports. Most Australians are.'

'I'm not bad,' he conceded as they reached the taxi
rank and stopped. 'When it comes to surfing, sailing
and swimming, I can give any guy a run for his money.'

Conscious of Alex almost abreast of them, she laughed
up at Kevin as if he had uttered the most brilliant joke,
and lightly placed her hand on his arm. 'Don't keep
staring at Fiona with sheep's eyes,' she advised under
her breath. 'Girls don't go for men who are push-overs.'

'Yes, ma'am. I'll take note of what you say!'

The beach house where they were staying was exactly as
Alex had described it. Set on the edge of silver-white
sand, bordered on one side by an azure sea and on the
other by waving green palms, its wood exterior bleached
pale grey by the tropical sun, it had the air of having
grown on the shore and not been built by man.

The interior was simple but luxurious: creamy fabrics spiced with royal blue and yellow, bamboo easy-chairs softened by thick feather cushions, Western-style furniture in the dining alcove and bedrooms, and colourful rugs on the teak floors. The kitchen was small but well equipped and, best of all, was presided over by Sumalee, a dainty, sweet-faced girl who informed them, in halting English, that she was there to take care of them.

'You should ask your friend if we can have this place for our honeymoon, Alex.' Fiona dropped on to a lounger on the veranda. 'It's perfect.'

'It certainly is,' he said shortly. 'But right now let's decide on our rooms. I suggest you girls take the two facing the sea.'

Kevin picked up his case and Marly's. 'I'm for a swim as soon as I've unpacked my gear.'

'Me too,' she agreed.

'And me,' Fiona volunteered, slipping past Marly and heading for the bedroom furthest from the living-room.

Because it afforded her more privacy should Alex decide to spend time in it? Marly conjectured, an idea which left a distinctly nasty taste in her mouth. Swallowing hard, she went into the other sea-view room and quickly changed into a one-piece cerise swimsuit.

Pity she couldn't wear one of her many bikinis, she mused as she twisted her hair into a single plait down her back, entwining it with a matching ribbon, for though she was petite, her body was beautifully formed, with delicate curves and roundness, and full, high breasts. But a well brought-up Thai woman would be happier in a one-piece, preferring to be seen in a garment that left more to the imagination!

Alex, to judge by his reaction when he saw her, had a highly active imagination. He was alone on the veranda when she went out, and at sight of her his lower lip moved sensuously, as if he were tasting her. For her part, she was equally bemused at seeing him in the most minimal of swimming-trunks. The width of his shoulders, she realised, had nothing to do with skilfully padded jackets, his narrow waist curved into well muscled thighs, and his long legs were strong and lean. The tangle of hair she had glimpsed on his chest through the open neck of his sports shirt was, she now saw, thick and silky, and a paler gold than his bronzed skin.

'You're more exquisite than I imagined,' he said throatily, grey irises darkening as they rested on the thrusting fullness of her breasts.

As if he had touched them, her nipples hardened and pushed forward against the silky material covering them. He saw it and took a step towards her, stopping abruptly as Fiona waltzed out.

'How do I look?' she asked gaily, twirling in front of him. 'Mature enough for us to set our wedding date?'

'We must have the two loveliest women in Phuket staying in this villa,' he grinned and, ignoring the second part of the question, put his hand to his head and added, 'But how do I handle two gorgeous women at the same time?'

'You don't. Leave Marly to Kevin, and you just handle *me*!'

'From the way Kevin's been eyeing you, I think he'd prefer the opposite.'

Fiona giggled. 'In that case, the question is how do *I* handle two handsome men?'

The man they had been discussing came round the side of the beach house and dashed across the sand towards the sea. Though not as well built as Alex, he was equally muscular. Red-blond hair flying, and with a boyish grin on his even-featured face, he cavorted in the waves like a schoolboy, calling to everyone to join him.

Marly did, anxious to cool off in more ways than one! The sea was a delight, crystal-clear and buoyant, and she dived and came up and dived again, hoping to wash away the sight of Fiona clinging to Alex and squealing like a frightened child. Recollecting the expertise with which the girl had swum in the hotel pool, Marly could happily have throttled her! Then she stared at Alex whose strong arms were supporting the slender frame, and could have throttled him instead! Why was he pandering to her silly nonsense? He should disengage himself and swim smartly away. Or perhaps he didn't really want to leave her side?

Diving beneath the waves, Marly came up close to Kevin. 'Break up the twosome, would you, before I throw up?'

Kevin flung her a startled glance, then swam across to Fiona, who was still playing her frightened-little-girl act. 'I can't believe a fabulous swimmer like you is frightened of the sea,' he said heartily, before addressing Alex. 'We had a race in the hotel pool and this little beaut almost beat me!'

'So you finally conquered your fear of going out of your depth?' Alex exclaimed, and swung her high in the air.

'I was going to tell you in a minute,' she squealed.

'Now there's no need,' he laughed, and dropped her into the water. Before she could surface, he did a fast crawl over to Marly. 'Let's leave them to it,' he said, and catching her hand, waded with her on to the beach.

Expecting Fiona to hurry after them, she was delighted to see that Kevin had persuaded her to race him to the raft, moored a hundred or so yards out to sea.

'I do believe Kevin's going to be a blessing,' Alex drawled, drawing Marly down on to the sand.

Whether by luck or judgement, he had chosen a spot that was hidden from sight of the swimmers, shaded as it was by a cluster of baby palms. Marly's pulses were racing so fast that she was afraid Alex would see the beat of them on her skin, and she hastily sank down and swung over on to her stomach.

His hand lightly caressed the delicate bones of her spine. 'You're so fragile,' he said huskily, 'I'm afraid of crushing you.'

She was aware of his head lowering, but was taken aback when she felt his tongue lapping the length of her spine. Momentarily she allowed herself to believe this scene was for real: that Alex was sincere, and that there was no Andrea or Fiona in the background. For as long as possible she tried to hold on to the fantasy, but truth would not be denied and, anxious to escape the dangerous touch of his hands, she slid away from them and turned on to her back.

She knew instantly it was the wrong thing to have done, for it brought him into all too clear focus, and she could not drag her gaze from the magnificent sight of him: the trunks that clung to him as if they were a second skin, the rippling bronzed muscles, the droplets of water on the thick lashes fringing eyes that were hungrily absorbing her.

A deep sigh escaped her, which he was quick to hear. 'What's wrong, Marly? That was a sad sound.'

'It was one of relief,' she denied, cursing his perception. 'Relief at being away from my computer.'

'And gladness to be with me?'

'Fishing for compliments?'

'You're the only girl I've had to do it with,' he confessed ruefully. 'You make me so damned uncertain.'

'About what?'

'Our relationship. What you think of me.'

Triumph shot through her. 'Is it important?'

'Let me show you how important.'

He pressed his lips on hers, and her first thought was that they were exactly as she had imagined: cool, firm, yet with a hint of fire. Determined to maintain her shy behaviour, she tried to turn her face aside, but steel fingers prevented her as his kiss deepened. Desperately she willed herself not to respond, but though she could control her lips, keep her arms at her sides and stop her body arching into his, she could not control the pounding of her heart, the leap of her pulses, nor the mounting passion that heated her and brought glittering drops of perspiration to the shadowed valley between her breasts.

'Open your mouth,' he commanded beneath his breath.

For answer she kept it tightly closed, and he cupped either side of her face with his hands. 'When the princess kissed the toad he turned into a handsome prince!' Alex whispered, the thickness of his voice indicative of his arousal. 'The same thing might happen to me if you kiss me back!'

'You're already a handsome prince!' she said, deciding humour was the best way of dissolving his ardour. 'If I do as you ask, the process might be reversed and you could turn *into* a toad!'

Alex chuckled and released her. 'You enjoy making fun of me, don't you?'

'It's good for you.' She sat up straight. 'It stops you getting too conceited.'

'Fat chance of that with you around. For someone who looks a shy little girl, you talk back in a very adult way!'

'Should I take that as a compliment?'

'Take what as a compliment?' The question came from Fiona, who was looming above them, and then sank down on the sand beside Alex.

'I was telling Marly how pleased I am with the program she's done for the hotel,' he stated with commendable aplomb.

'You and business,' Fiona pouted prettily. 'Don't you ever think of anything else?'

'Not when you're around!'

Marly listened to the banter with irritation, as did Kevin, who had now joined them. Why did Alex continue to play up to the girl if his intention was to escape her clutches?

'You pay me the sweetest compliments,' Fiona beamed, resting her bright blonde head on his shoulder. 'However much of a hard-head you are in business, you're always such a softie with me.'

'Most men would be the same, given the opportunity,' Kevin grinned. 'You should try it some time.'

'The only man I want is Alex—so save your flattery for Marly. Otherwise she'll feel she's a third wheel.'

'I doubt Marly could ever feel that,' Alex interpolated drily. 'She's not exactly a member of the ugly club!' He leaned back on the sand, arms behind his head. 'Where do you folks want to go for dinner? A restaurant, or have it here on the beach?'

'On the beach,' Fiona said excitedly. 'It will be like that advert on TV where the couple sit at a table by the water's edge, and the candlelight rivals the moon.' She glanced at Marly. 'Would you arrange it with Sumalee? I can't speak Thai, and I don't think her English is good enough for her to understand *my* instructions.'

Glad of the chance of escaping, Marly gracefully rose and went into the beach house. It didn't take her long to explain to Sumalee what was wanted, and after a menu had been agreed she chose not to return to the beach but retired to her room, where she showered, slipped into a cotton robe and lay on the bed, trying not to think of Alex.

What a hope when she could think of nothing else! If today was a forerunner of the rest of the week, she would be lost to reason long before this trip was over. Snap out of it, she ordered herself. If you can't control your emotions, do as Nan suggested and come clear with him. Say the whole thing was a joke and that you've grown tired of it. Yet as the idea entered her head she dismissed it as a cop-out, a sign of her weakness. And she wasn't weak. She was a liberated woman in charge of her feelings; upon which thought she picked up one of the books she had brought with her and determinedly concentrated on it.

The moon was a silver orb in a velvet dark sky when the four of them sat down to dinner on the veranda. Although their bamboo table wasn't lapped by the sea, it was close enough to the water for them to hear the soft slap of the gentle waves on the sand. Sumalee had prepared a veritable feast: lemon chicken soup, sweet and sour shrimp, fresh-water cod, lamb in coconut and green curry, and a huge bowl of fluffy white rice.

'We'll never get through this lot!' Fiona exclaimed.

But they did, and several desserts in addition.

'I don't know about the rest of you,' Alex murmured as, the table cleared, they returned to the veranda for coffee, 'but I've eaten so much that all I'm fit for is bed.'

'Me too,' Fiona said quickly, moving to his side.

Marly, aware of Alex eyeing her, made a great play of pouring herself some coffee. 'I'll stay put for a while,' she replied, reluctant to go in with him. If she was reading the glint in his eyes correctly, sleep was the furthest thing from his mind, and she was not certain how she would handle things if he came to her room.

Never had she been so physically attracted to a man, nor so tempted to forgo her principles and surrender to desire. Only the knowledge of why she was here—and that their whole relationship was based on a lie—gave her the strength to go on resisting him.

'I'll keep you company,' Kevin grunted, watching Fiona and Alex go inside, with the girl clinging to his arm. 'I'm not tired anyway.'

'I doubt if they are either,' Marly retorted.

'You don't think... Dammit, he wouldn't go to bed with her, would he? I thought you said he wants to be free of her, not encourage her!'

'Who knows what he'll do if he can't have *me*?' Marly replied with brutal honesty. 'She keeps throwing herself at him and he's only human.'

Kevin's face darkened. 'I think I'll go in after all.'

'And do what—stand guard outside her door? Relax and be fatalistic.'

'It's not easy. I've never felt this way before, but there's something about Fiona that... I've tried telling myself it's only physical attraction but I know it's more than that.'

'I'll see if I can think of a way of keeping Alex out of Fiona's life for a couple of days. That should at least give you a chance of making some impression on her.'

Kevin brightened. 'It would be great if you could manage it. I don't wish the guy any harm but a sprained ankle would be perfect!'

Marly laughed. 'I wasn't anticipating anything quite so drastic!'

Even as she spoke a plan formulated in her mind, and as soon as she was alone she saw how it could be accomplished. Born of desperation, for it was clear Alex was determined to remain single, it required a good deal of luck, and would not only stretch her acting ability but be the ultimate test of her will-power.

Yet if it worked she would not merely achieve her aims, but Kevin's as well, for it would drive Fiona straight into his arms, and Alex into her own!

CHAPTER TEN

'THERE'S a yacht club near by,' Alex announced over breakfast on the veranda next morning. 'So if anyone cares for a game of squash or tennis——'

'I wouldn't mind playing tennis,' Fiona said.

'I'll second that,' Kevin put in promptly.

In pastel floral wrap-around skirt and matching lawn top, the young blonde had the soft, fragrant look of a dew-fresh bloom, and as she gazed adoringly at Alex, Marly's heart lurched. Had they spent the night together? He certainly looked as if he hadn't slept much. His face lacked its usual healthy glow and there were noticeable lines around his eyes. Not that this lessened his sexual attraction—far from it—for it set her imagination alight, causing all kinds of erotic pictures to float into her mind.

'How about you, Alex?' Fiona enquired.

'I think I'll give it a miss. I didn't sleep too well last night.'

'Then I'll stay and keep you company.'

'That will defeat the object. How can I sleep if you're keeping me company?'

'I'll be quiet as a mouse.'

'I've heard that one before!' With a resigned sigh, he pushed back his chair. 'OK, count me in. Are you going to join us, Marly?'

'I didn't bring any tennis gear,' she replied truthfully. Apart from it being a game she preferred to watch rather than play, the plan she had formulated last night meant separating Alex from Fiona. And for that she had to stay behind.

'Fiona has a spare racket,' he said, 'and there's a sports shop at the club where you can get kitted out—my treat.'

'Thank you, but no. I couldn't accept such a present.'

'It won't be from me personally,' he added swiftly. 'It's a gift from the company in appreciation of your hard work.'

'I'm sufficiently well paid for it.'

Alex looked as if he wanted to argue, then a glint came into his eye and he swung round to Fiona. 'Looks as if you and Kevin will have to play a singles match. I'll stay and keep Marly company.'

'Don't be silly, darling,' Fiona expostulated. 'I'm sure Marly doesn't want to spoil our game, and there's bound to be someone at the club willing to make a fourth.'

'Fiona's right,' Marly put in sweetly. 'And to be honest, I'd prefer to sunbathe and swim.' She raised her arms and stretched, aware that the gesture provocatively thrust forward her small, pointed breasts. 'It's so deserted here I might even pluck up the courage and go topless.' She studied his reaction from beneath lowered lashes, and wondered if he would fall for the bait.

If he had, he was giving nothing away, and with a lift of his hand he went in to collect his racket and shoes.

Finishing her breakfast, Marly headed for the dock, where Alex's friend moored his cabin cruiser. It was sleek and beautiful, its paint sparkling, its brass gleaming. Quickly she slipped aboard and padded over to the engine. Her parents and brothers were keen sailors, and she had been brought up with a love and knowledge of the sea and boats. Consequently, setting the first part of her plan in motion presented no difficulty, and when she had accomplished it she returned to the beach house.

Fifteen minutes later, in yellow two-piece swimsuit and dark glasses, she emerged to wander along the beach, where she soon spread her towel in the shade of a palm tree. Long silky hair loose about her, and the latest bestseller unopened beside her, she lay on her stomach and unhooked the top of her suit. A faint breeze stirred the air, bringing the salt scent of the ocean to her nostrils, and she breathed in deeply and closed her eyes, only realising as she did so what a strain it was becoming to maintain her charade. Tension drained from her and, as she relaxed, her true self emerged and all pretences dropped away from her so that Alex could have seen her as she really was.

'Marly,' a deep voice whispered softly.

She stirred but did not lift her lids, for if she did, reality would return and Alex would fade away.

'Marly,' the voice said again, and this time her eyes flew open and she turned her head and saw Alex kneeling beside her.

With a gasp she reached her hands behind her to do up her swimsuit, at the same time trying to remain flat on the sand. But her fingers seemed to have turned to thumbs, and she was still struggling with the hooks when firm, cool fingers did the job for her.

Only then did she sit up and swivel round to face him, and saw that he was in swimming-trunks, that his legs were strong and lean, his eyes warm grey, the smile he gave her meltingly intimate.

'How come you're back so soon?' She marvelled that her voice came out so cool.

'I developed a sudden headache!'

'I thought that was the prerogative of married women!'

'As a reluctant fiancé I feel I qualify!'

Hiding her triumph at his return, Marly toyed idly with her sunglasses. 'Do you think Fiona believed you?'

'Does it matter?'

'One should always consider other people's feelings,' she answered demurely. 'Thai philosophy——'

'No lectures, please,' he said with mock severity. 'I wanted to be alone with you and I think that's what you wanted too. In fact, you deliberately tried to tempt me back, didn't you?' Slate eyes glinted with humour. 'You appear to have had second thoughts about the bait, though. Clearly your sense of modesty got the better of you.'

She could not stop the blush that stained her cheeks, and avoided his eyes. Normally not a shy girl, she had occasionally gone topless when sunbathing with friends, yet the thought of doing so with Alex made her feel strangely vulnerable.

'Pity,' he said with a shake of his head. 'You have beautiful breasts, and it's a shame to cover them.'

Silently she tipped suntan lotion into her palms and began to rub it on her shoulders and arms.

'Need any help?' he asked, squatting down beside her.

'No, thanks.'

'Frightened one thing will lead to another?'

'Frankly, yes.'

His mouth quirked. 'Then how about a swim to cool us both off?'

'I've an even cooler idea,' she answered, as if the thought had suddenly occurred to her, instead of being part of the plan she had formulated last night. 'How about taking out the boat to one of the islands? That way we can have the whole morning to ourselves, instead of just a couple of hours until the others return.'

'Brilliant! But better still, why don't we take a picnic and make a day of it? We'll leave a note for Fiona and Kevin—he'll be delighted of course—and perhaps by the time we get back she won't be averse to him either.'

Marly shook her head. 'I can't see Fiona giving up on you that easily. She's been obsessive about you for too long.'

'Now you're spoiling my day.' He rose and pulled her to her feet. 'Come on, let's ask Sumalee to prepare a picnic for us.'

'I'll do it. You write the note to Fiona.'

In no time Marly had a basket packed with sufficient goodies to last a couple of days, and pausing only to pack a few things in her beach bag, she joined Alex on the veranda.

'I brought along a couple of bottles of Donald's best New Zealand Chardonnay,' he informed her, pointing to the leather wine-cooler on the seat next to him. 'Sailing is thirsty work!'

'Particularly on a boat that's motor-powered!' she laughed.

'Don't quibble about semantics. To me, one boat is like another!'

'I hope that doesn't mean you don't know anything about them?' she questioned, trying to look anxious. 'I'd hate to break down mid-ocean and have to swim back. These waters are shark-infested.'

'Don't worry. I may not be round-the-world material, but I'm not a complete novice.' He half smiled. 'The boat's just had an overhaul, and Donald told me the engine's as reliable as a Rolls.'

'Shall we get going, then?'

Side by side they strolled down to the slatted wooden dock where the two-berth cabin cruiser rocked gently on the swell. Named *Lovely Linda* in bold black letters on the freshly painted white hull, the boat flew an American flag.

'Who's "Lovely Linda"?' Marly asked curiously as they went aboard. 'Your friend's wife?'

'Ex,' Alex corrected. 'But he's still in love with her and doesn't want to change the name.'

'Why did they divorce, then?'

'You make it sound as if the man's always the one to want out,' Alex was quick to say, reminding Marly yet again how sharp he was.

'They usually are,' she said.

'Not this time. The not so lovely Linda ran off with her tennis coach.'

'Then I'd have thought the last thing your friend would want was to be reminded of her.'

Alex shrugged. 'Love is like a drug addiction—once hooked, hard to cure.'

'Is that experience talking?'

'I've never touched drugs.'

'I was talking about love,' Marly said demurely.

'Let's talk about *that* later,' he grinned, and disappeared into the galley to put the picnic and the wine into the refrigerator.

While Marly set out two sunbeds, Alex busied himself at the wheel. Effortlessly the powerful engine surged into life, and casting off the line he slowly edged the boat away from the dock. Once clear, he increased the speed, set it on automatic pilot and joined Marly.

'Care for a drink?' he questioned.

'It's only eleven-thirty.'

'There's no law that says we have to wait until the sun's over the yard-arm.'

She wrinkled her brow, pretending not to understand. 'I'm afraid I don't know that expression.'

'That you don't drink alcohol until after noon,' he explained.

'After noon?' Marly raised her eyebrows. 'I usually wait until after six!'

'In that case I shall enjoy corrupting you at one minute past twelve!'

True to his word, noon found them sipping a delicious fruity Chardonnay as they lay under the canvas awning and stared out at the sparkling blue sea. The sky seemed to reflect its colour, Marly thought, or was it the other way around? Either way it was a blue, blue world, with the sun a golden orb dredging them with its warmth.

Soon the insidiousness of the heat dissipated their conversation, bringing with it a blissful languor. Turning her head to remark on this, Marly saw that Alex had fallen asleep with the suddenness of a child. It gave her the chance to study him without being observed, and she enjoyed the handsome picture he made. His face in repose was younger and carefree, making him appear defenceless, the strong lines around his mouth softened into gentleness, and she had only to inch out her fingers to feel the burnished hairs on his arm. She longed to do so, but wary of awakening him, she resisted the temptation, and with a small sigh closed her eyes and drifted into slumber.

She awoke with a feeling of being watched, and opening her eyes found Alex propped on one elbow, looking into her face.

'Pleasant dreams?' he asked.

'I wasn't asleep,' she denied. 'Just dozing.'

'From the baby piglet sounds you were making, you could have fooled me!'

'If you're implying I was snoring...' she said indignantly.

'There's no implying about it,' he grinned. 'I was stating a fact! Don't get uptight, though. On you it sounded like a Mozart symphony!'

Marly laughed. 'I thought love was blind, not *deaf*!'

'After two glasses of wine and the heat of the sun, *all* my faculties are impaired!'

'Good. I finally feel safe with you.'

Chuckling, he rose. 'Let's have lunch. That will sober me.' As she went to rise, he shook his head. 'No, stay where you are. I can manage on my own.'

'You're spoiling me.'

'I'd like to do much more than that,' he said thickly, and half bent towards her, then seeing her sudden tension he drew back and went below deck.

Within a few moments he returned with the food, which he deftly set out on a white, slatted wood table. There was a delicious Thai salad—a mix of succulent prawns, lobster claws, spring onions and tiny white aubergines resembling new potatoes—a dish of deep-fried chicken wings with soy sauce and pineapple, a bowl of rice, and another piled high with mangoes and papayas.

The wonderful mix of aromas made Marly realise how hungry she was, and she sat at the table and helped herself to the food.

'Where exactly are we headed?' she asked, tucking in to the prawns.

'Kwin Yak. We should arrive there in about forty minutes.'

Marly knew it was one of the larger islands and, like the others, uninhabited. Which suited her purpose beautifully.

'I'm longing for a swim,' she said, 'and after a lunch like this I'll need it to burn off some calories.'

Alex shook his head. 'You don't seem to gain weight however much you eat—and you have a pretty hefty appetite for a dainty little thing.'

'I never gain weight.'

He pulled a face, and his expression drew her eyes to his body, making her aware of the hard muscles of his chest, the flatness of his stomach, the tensile strength of his long legs, the sun-kissed golden skin. A burning heat suffused her and she hastily set down her fork lest he noticed the tremble of her hands.

'I remember you said you used to have a weight problem,' she managed to say.

'I did as a youngster, but that was because I stuffed myself with candy bars. I was at boarding-school, and the food was so dull, I made up for it with chocolates and sweets.'

'How did you kick the habit?' Marly grinned.

'It was after I fell in love with my best friend's sister—Sandra, you remember?—and asked her to marry me. She rejected me in favour of a long, thin streak of a lad with a laugh like a hyena!'

'I bet that didn't do any good for your ego!' Marly giggled. 'Did you have better luck once you'd slimmed down?'

'With the fickleness of youth, I lost interest—and weight—and went on to pastures new. But we became good friends and I'm godfather to her eldest son.'

'And your rival?'

'She married him!' Alex helped himself to another piece of chicken. 'He was highly successful in the City by then.'

'Have you never wanted to marry anyone since?' Marly ventured with forced casualness.

'For a shy young lady you ask some leading questions,' he said drily. 'But the answer's no.'

'Because you've never been in love, or you don't want to tie yourself down?'

His lower lip jutted forward, as if considering the questions. 'Why commit oneself to one woman when the world is full of lovely ones ripe for the picking?'

'And unlike wives, they can be changed if you get bored,' Marly added sweetly.

'You've hit the nail on the head.'

And how, she thought bitterly, and wished she could hit *him* on the head instead!

'You might change your opinion one day. This year's playboy is next year's dirty old man!'

'Well said.' Alex's face was alight with amusement. 'But luckily for me I'd rather be a dirty old man than a cheating husband. At least that way the only person I deceive is myself.'

'If you met the right woman you——'

'Spare me that cliché. Conversion by true love is the classic reply of the fair sex! You surprise me, Marly. Until now you've always talked in a very practical, logical manner, but it seems that you're a closet romantic!'

Marly saw nothing funny in his comment, her mind's eye filled with Andrea's tear-stained face. 'At least I have a heart,' she replied.

'So have I when it comes to family and friends,' he defended. 'I'm a loving son, a loyal confidant, and a passionate lover.' Slate eyes glinted mischievously. 'If you don't believe the latter, I'd be more than happy to prove it.'

'I'll take your word for it, thanks. There's no sense in being one of a number, when what I really want is to be number one!'

His smile was sensuous, the full lower lip curving forward. 'I find your wit enjoyable, Marly. Pity you're so old-fashioned.'

'It's because I'm different from the other girls you know that I hold your interest.'

'You think so?' With a gentle finger he traced the perfect line of her cheekbone. 'I'd be interested in you even if you were as liberated as Gloria Steinem!' His hand rose and touched her silky hair. 'You're very special.'

'Special enough to marry?' she asked ingenuously.

'You have a one-track mind,' he chuckled, dropping his hand abruptly.

'So have you. But yours is trying to lead me up the garden path, and mine is keeping me on the straight and narrow!' Deftly she put the used plates on a tray and placed the bowl of fruit between them. 'Shall I peel you a mango or would you prefer a papaya?'

If he was surprised by her sudden change of tack he gave no sign of it, though as she continued prattling on about nothing, the withdrawn look in his eyes convinced her he wasn't concentrating on what she was saying.

Clearly she had given him food for thought, and if Lady Luck was on her side, he might not find it too indigestible!

CHAPTER ELEVEN

THE sun was at its zenith when Alex and Marly reached the island and laid anchor in Kwin Yak's small, deserted bay. Froth-edged waves gently lapped the coastline, and the water was startlingly clear with tiny, silvery fish swimming just below the surface.

The beach was powder-white, and the sand felt like silk upon their bare feet as they paddled to the shore in a small rubber dinghy and dropped their towels beneath the shade of a small clump of palm trees, their shaggy fronds waving in the faint breeze.

'Fancy a swim before we explore?' Alex suggested.

Nodding, she followed him into the water, and hardly had she immersed herself when he took her hand and drew her further into the azure-blue sea. Together they set off in the direction of the boat, swimming lazily in line with it and then heading back to dry off on the warm sand.

'I feel as if we're the last two people left on earth,' Marly said breathlessly as, a little later, they strolled along the beach. 'This must be the most peaceful place on earth.'

'Pity we have to go back tonight,' Alex commented. 'I suppose I can't persuade you to stay?'

'You suppose right,' she replied, managing to hide her amusement as she thought of the skilful way she had sabotaged the engine to ensure it wouldn't start. 'And don't try the old chestnut about not being able to start the boat!'

'You misjudge me,' he reproached her. 'Don't you trust me?'

'No!'

He laughed. 'You're a strange mixture of docility and sassiness.'

'That's a Thai characteristic. On the surface we're sweetness and light, but underneath we have a will of our own.'

'You rarely display it with *me*.'

'Because you're my superior.'

'Only at the hotel. In our personal relationship we are equals.'

'We can never be that,' she persisted, playing her role to the hilt. 'You are an important man and I will always defer to you.'

'What if we were married?' he teased.

'Especially then.'

Alex chuckled. 'I can see you will make an excellent wife!'

'Are *you* proposing to me, Alex?' She fluttered her long lashes at him.

'Any proposal I made wouldn't be for marriage,' he responded good-humouredly, 'though you deserve an A plus for persistence.'

'And you deserve an A plus for *resistance*!'

They had now returned to the spot where their towels lay, and they relaxed in the warmth for an hour and then rowed back to the boat, both absorbed in their thoughts and content to remain silent. It had been a perfect day, Marly conceded, and was reluctant for it to end, wishing to hold on to the idyll for as long as possible.

Knowing what was going to happen, and worried she might not be able to play the innocent, she busied herself in the galley making coffee while Alex went off to start the engine. It roared into life and then frustratingly died—not surprising given that she had earlier ensured that the engine's vibration would loosen one of the main leads sufficiently to cause a fuse when the engine was stopped and then restarted. It was easy enough to repair, but even if Alex was a whiz with engines he would take some time to locate the fault, and by then it would be dark and inadvisable to attempt the return journey.

After she had heard him make several unsuccessful attempts to fire the motor, she decided it might seem odd if she didn't show some curiosity, and she hurried on deck to join him.

'Anything wrong?' she cooed.

'Yes, but I'm damned if I can see what it is.'

Watching him tug at wires, test screws, and tinker around with a spanner, it was clear to Marly, who had a good knowledge of engines, that in spite of looking as if he knew what he was doing Alex knew very little.

'Don't tell me we've run out of fuel?' she asked straight-faced as he wiped his grease-stained fingers on an oily rag.

'I won't—because we haven't,' he stated edgily.

'Can it be the fan belt, then?'

'You'll be asking about the exhaust next,' he muttered. 'This isn't a car, you know!'

'Sorry. I was only trying to help.'

'Then see if you can find the instruction manual. I noticed it below somewhere.'

She found it on top of some books in the main cabin, and pretending not to notice it was printed in Japanese, solemnly handed it to him.

Alex riffled through the pages and swore softly under his breath, though sufficient words were audible to bring the colour to her cheeks, a fact he noticed immediately.

'Forgive me, Marly, but this is absolutely useless. Unless *you* speak Japanese?'

'Fluently,' she said drily. 'Toyota, Mitsubishi, Honda, Sony——'

'Very funny,' he cut in. 'But this is no joking matter. I'll have to radio for help, though I doubt if the coast-guard will launch a rescue this late in the day, as we aren't in any danger.'

'Why are you so certain you can't fix it?' she asked, putting deep suspicion into her voice. 'You told me you knew about boats.'

'I know about cars too, but that doesn't mean I'm an expert. There's obviously a serious fault and it will take a professional to repair it.'

'You said your friend just had the boat checked and that it was as safe as a Rolls-Royce,' she accused.

'Clearly he was wrong.'

'It isn't clear to me,' she sniffed indignantly. 'Are you sure you didn't tamper with the engine so we'd be stuck here for the night?'

Alex straightened, his features rigid with controlled anger. 'I'm not some sex-starved youth who needs to trick a girl into spending the night with him. If you don't believe me, I suggest you take a look at the engine and see if *you* can see what's wrong with it.'

'You're on safe ground there. I wouldn't know what's wrong if the fault were painted striped pink and green!' she lied.

'Then I suggest you resign yourself to spending the night here with me,' he said in clipped tones, and dis-appeared to radio for help.

Stifling her laughter, Marly wandered across to the rail. It was a clear and beautiful night, the dark sky pep-pered with stars, a full moon casting a silver stairway across the sea. If only this night were for real, and Alex a man she could believe in and love, not someone who took what he could and then moved on to pastures new.

'It's as I assumed,' his deep voice said from behind her, and she tensed but did not move as he joined her at the rail. 'Once the coastguard ascertained we weren't in danger, they said we'd have to wait till morning.'

'I see.'

'Don't be upset, Marly. We may get hungry but——'

'We won't. There's plenty of food left,' she said, having planned it that way.

'Good. And we can wash it down with champagne. I found some in a locker and put it in the fridge.'

'While it's cooling, I'll have a shower,' she said.

'So will I—after you, of course!'

Standing in the tiny shower cubicle, Marly congratulated herself on how well everything had gone so far. But the most difficult part was to come. Alone with a man to whom she was strongly attracted on a physical level—and when he was not behaving like a chauvinist pig, on a cerebral one too—she planned to let him make love to her and then halt the proceedings mid-track. Just far enough, in fact, to show him the delights available to him if he married her. It was a trick as old as the hills and he might be wise to it, but given that she could not think of anything better, it was a gamble worth taking, for if he did finally propose, her revenge would be even sweeter than she had anticipated.

Slipping on silk panties and not bothering with a bra, she donned the white silk cheong-sam she had brought with her in her beach bag. The top was cut tight—as it always was—and showed a tantalising expanse of silky skin from just under her breasts to her waist, and the skirt clung lovingly to the rounded curves of her hips, a long slit in the side parting as she moved, to show a tantalising length of shapely leg.

Content with her image, she liberally sprayed herself with Giorgio. This should make Alex's temperature rise. She only hoped she had the strength of mind to lower

it before it rocketed out of control and sent her soaring
with him!

Perspiration dampened her brow at the very notion,
and she pushed her hair away from her face. Brushed
until it shone, it tumbled like a sheet of satin over her
shoulders. Totally without conceit, she knew she had
never looked lovelier or more desirable. Her slight tan
enhanced the pure white of her cheong-sam, and today's
surfeit of sun had heightened the colour in her cheeks,
giving them a rosy glow.

Alex, who was waiting outside, towel in hand, stared
at her transfixed, and she heard the catch of his breath.

'You're exquisite,' he said huskily, stepping into the
shower-room. 'Don't grow wings and fly away.'

'Chance would be a fine thing!'

His chuckle followed her as she went up on deck. He
had found a couple of deckchairs, and on the slatted
table that they had used for their lunch he had set out
the food for their dinner, covering it with a fine lawn
cloth to keep it fresh. She pulled a face. He might not
be husband material, but he was definitely house-trained!
Was that because of his hotel experience or because he
frequently had live-in lovers? Nervousness assailed her
and she fought it down, aware that if she didn't, Alex's
antenna was well tuned enough to sense it.

His step sounded behind her and she swung round to
see him walking towards her, a champagne bottle in one
hand, corkscrew and two fluted glasses in the other. In
brief shorts and matching Gucci cotton sports shirt the
colour of freshly churned butter, he was every girl's idea
of Prince Charming.

'It's the real thing,' he smiled, holding up the bottle
for her to see it was vintage Krug. Setting it on the table,
he deftly uncorked it, filled the two glasses and handed
her a foaming one. 'To us,' he toasted. 'May this night
together be the first of many.'

Refusing to acknowledge the implication behind the seemingly innocent words, she touched her glass to his. 'May we sleep in our beds tomorrow!'

Alex's lips were curled into a smile as he raised the glass rim to his mouth and drank, and with a shiver of apprehension Marly knew that the task she had set herself was fraught with danger.

'Delicious champagne,' she observed.

'For a delicious woman. "Here's looking at you shweetheart,"' he added in a fair imitation of Humphrey Bogart's famous line in *Casablanca*.

'You've missed your vocation,' she smiled.

'I doubt that. My only other recognisable impersonation is Donald Duck!'

They exchanged glances of amusement, and their eyes met and held; hers nut-brown and wary; his silver-grey and getting darker as they ranged over the smooth oval of her face, slender neck, and small, full breasts.

'Do I take it you're a movie buff?' she asked, anxious to keep the conversation on an impersonal level for as long as possible.

'Not especially. I prefer the theatre.'

'So do I.'

'What's it like in Thailand?'

She was momentarily flummoxed. Not having been, she had absolutely no idea. 'Not in the same class as London or New York,' she cleverly parried, then hurriedly switched the discussion to music.

In this, his taste was similar to hers, and they debated the merits of jazz and blues, rock and rap, and musicals. Only when it came to opera and classical music did their tastes diverge, for he liked ultra-modern composers and she preferred Mozart, Brahms, and Verdi. But again she deferred to him, nodding sagely when he expounded on the merits of an avant-garde composer she found particularly atonal.

'Don't you find the Second Movement of his Fourth Symphony brilliant?' Alex questioned.

'Brilliant,' she echoed.

'Liar.'

'*What*?'

'I said liar,' Alex answered pleasantly. 'There isn't a Second Movement because there isn't a Fourth Symphony. He's only written three!'

Furious with herself for falling into such a simple trap, Marly lowered her head. 'I'm sorry, Alex. I didn't like to admit my ignorance.'

'You mean you didn't want to admit you don't like modern composers. Why not, for heaven's sake?'

'It's a matter of taste, I suppose.'

'That's obvious,' he said tersely, 'but it isn't what I meant! I'm just curious to know why you wouldn't disagree with me.'

'It isn't seemly.'

Alex visibly swallowed a retort and Marly awarded herself full marks for riling him the way she had. Not so many weeks ago he had professed himself delighted with her amiable disposition, but now he was beginning to see how irritating a 'yes-woman' could be. By the time she finished with him, he would make sure that his next love-affair was with a rampant feminist!

Deciding to change the subject, she began removing the covers from the food. 'I don't know about you, but I could eat a horse.'

'I'd rather ride them,' he said with a return to good humour. 'But I wouldn't refuse a little something else.'

In the event he ate a big something else, tucking into his food with gusto. 'There's nothing nicer than dining at sea with a beautiful woman,' he sighed contentedly. 'Even Anton Mosiman couldn't have bettered it!'

'Anton Mosiman?' She feigned ignorance.

'He's one of the finest chefs I know. He runs his own restaurant in London. I'd like to take you there some time.'

She restrained the urge to tell him she occasionally dined there. 'I have no plans to visit your country.'

'Who knows what the future may hold?' he said softly.

She waited for him to elaborate, and when he didn't, knew he was mouthing words without meaning them. Typical of a man on the make!

'I shouldn't imagine you're very domesticated,' he went on unexpectedly.

'I happen to be a good cook—and tidy with it!'

A tawny eyebrow rose. 'From the little I've learned of Thai society, I was under the impression that most well-to-do families had domestic help.'

This was true, and too late Marly realised she had answered his question as herself, and not in the role she was portraying. Luckily it wasn't too late to retrieve the situation.

'You're right, Alex. None of my friends sets foot in her kitchen, but since I love food and am curious by nature, I took some cookery lessons.'

'When may I sample your efforts?'

'When my parents return and I move back home.'

There was a lengthy silence which Marly had no intention of breaking, and when she saw Alex didn't intend to do so either, she stacked the dirty dishes and glasses on a tray.

'Coffee?' she enquired, one foot on the rung of the steps leading to the galley.

'Please.'

The kettle was still boiling when Alex loomed large beside her. 'Anything I can do for you?'

If she was correctly interpreting the vibes he was emanating, coffee was the last thing he had in mind.

'How kind of you to ask,' she flattered.

'I can be kind in other ways too,' he answered throatily, and coming closer wound his fingers in her silky black hair, tilted her face up to his and laid claim to her mouth.

The insistent pressure of his lips forced hers apart, and instantly his tongue, hot and demanding, probed the inner softness, crashing through her defences and leaving her open to his demands. Again and again he drank deep of her, and unable—nay, unwilling—to resist him, she responded with all the ardour of which she was capable.

Alex was the first to draw back, stroking her cheek with a hand that trembled. 'You've cast a spell on me, darling,' he murmured. 'You've cast a spell on me and there's only one way to break it!'

Once more his mouth found hers and she made a show of attempting to break free, but even had she genuinely wished to do so it would have been useless, for his grip was like iron though his lips were velvet-soft as they traced tiny kisses down her throat to the soft curve of her breasts, the outline of her taut nipples clearly visible beneath the white silk cheong-sam.

Desire shot through her, piercing as a knife, and with a gasp she pushed against him, her palms flat upon his shoulders. This was Act One, and she had to play her part carefully.

'Please, Alex, let me go.'

Slowly he stepped back but kept his arms lightly around her. 'Why, my darling? You want me as much as I want you. We both knew it the moment we met, so why keep fighting it?'

Little did he know she had no intention of fighting it. No, sir, the name of the game was to drive him wild with longing and then pretend she was holding out for marriage.

Keeping her eyes downcast to hide the resolution in them, she put a tremor in her voice as she spoke. 'You know why I won't, Alex, and nothing has changed.'

'It has, darling. You love me. I've seen it in your look, heard it in your voice, felt it in your touch. Are you denying it?'

Cupping her face in his hands, he forced her eyes to meet his, and for what seemed an eternity they stared at one another. In the subdued lighting she saw the naked passion in his eyes and felt she was drowning in their depths, losing her sense of control.

'I can't deny it,' she answered shakily, and realising it was true, despised herself for it.

'Thank God you've finally admitted it!' Drawing her close, he stroked her shoulders and hips with practised ease, moulding his hands round the curve of her buttocks to press the lower part of her body upon the burgeoning swell of his arousal. 'I love you too,' he whispered against her throat. 'That's what makes it perfect.'

'I'm sure you've said that to other women.'

'You're wrong. I've teased and flattered and I've made love, but I haven't been *in* love. This is the first time and you are the first woman to whom I've said it.'

As the lies tripped from his tongue, the love within her dried up, and though it was painful to admit how unscrupulous he was, it made it easier for her to carry on with her plan.

'Alex, no!' she cried as he led her out of the galley. 'I can't. I'll regret it afterwards.'

'You won't, I promise you.' His head lowered to hers and his breath was warm as a summer breeze on her lips. 'I won't do anything to hurt you. Surely you know that?'

As one hackneyed phrase followed another, Marly's fury rose. Any moment now and he was going to come out with the old chestnut about stopping whenever she gave the word!

'You do trust me?' he asked thickly.

'Completely.'

It was all he needed, and lifting her into his arms he carried her effortlessly up to the deck.

Hardly had she time to absorb that while she had been in the galley preparing coffee he had rearranged the re-clining-chair cushions into a bed than she felt herself placed upon it and he was deftly undoing the tiny front buttons of her cheong-sam.

'You're perfect,' he whispered, releasing her breasts from the flimsy material and burying his face in the warm hollow between them. His tongue moved from one to the other, caressing the soft fullness before taking a hardened nipple in his mouth and sucking it.

A shaft of pure desire shot through her and every nerve in her body throbbed with ecstasy. Only then did her fear increase as she admitted that what he had said a moment ago was true: she wanted him as much as he wanted her.

But she dared not give in to him. To do so would send her into the same pit into which he had cast Andrea. She tried to pull away from him, but his hands held her prisoner as his lips parted hers, and her mouth gave up its moist sweetness to his marauding tongue. Feverishly she found herself responding to him, fatalistically ac-cepting the inevitable as he familiarised himself with every part of her naked body: rubbing, nibbling, stroking, sucking. The ache between her thighs was un-bearable, and more than anything else in the world she longed for his swollen hardness inside her. Now was the time to stop but her good intentions drowned in her need of him, and her legs parted spontaneously, telling him without words that only the ultimate act would satisfy her.

'Are you sure?' he muttered into her ear, momentarily easing his chest away from her breasts.

Surprised by his question, she wondered if he was playing Mr Nice Guy so that the onus for her seduction was firmly placed on her, rather than him. But even as she hesitated, lost in a moral dilemma and not certain which road to take, she heard the throb of an engine close by.

Alex heard it too, and jack-knifing into a sitting position, reached swiftly for their scattered clothes.

'*Pirates*?' she asked fearfully, bending low to stay out of sight as she put on her skirt.

'Not in this stretch of water. Either the coastguard changed their minds, or Fiona did it for them.' Alex slipped into his trousers and shirt and then stood up, masking her with his body. 'You should have a cheong-sam with a zip, not buttons!' He grinned briefly to lighten the mood. 'Bend double and go down below. I'll play host up here!'

Heart racing like a piston, she did as ordered, still so emotionally aroused that she was unable to think straight.

When she emerged, a sleek white cutter had pulled up alongside them and two coastguards were trying to explain their arrival to Alex, while a third was examining the engine, which burst into life even as Marly came forward to act as interpreter.

As Alex had correctly assumed, Fiona was the main instigator behind their rescue, for when an official had telephoned the beach house to explain their absence and say they would be rescued in the morning she had contacted the British embassy.

'The rest, as they say, is history,' Marly concluded as she recounted the story to Alex when the coastguards had returned to their vessel and were standing by to escort them back to Phuket. 'I don't think your fiancée is going to give up on you as easily as you think.'

'She is *not* my fiancée,' he asserted. 'This mania of hers is getting beyond a joke. If she carries on like this I'll have no option but to be brutal.'

'Not while she's such a long way from home,' Marly warned, cognisant of the girl's earlier breakdown. 'If our stay in Phuket doesn't show her you don't love her, it might be better if you flew back to England with her and then made her face the truth.'

Alex's grunt could have meant anything and Marly let the matter drop. After all, once she herself was finished with him, how he ran his life was no concern of hers.

The thought should have made her jump for joy, yet all it did was make her want to burst into tears. Which went to show what a stupid fool she was for having given her heart to a man who didn't have one of his own.

CHAPTER TWELVE

FIONA and Kevin were at the dockside waiting to welcome Alex and Marly when the boat slipped into its mooring place at two in the morning.

Fiona flung herself into Alex's arms with the fervour of a bride on the return of her husband from the battlefront, and though the display irritated Marly, she could not help but be grateful that the girl's determination to prevent him spending the night on the boat with another woman had prevented her from giving herself to Alex and making the biggest mistake of her life.

Pleading exhaustion, she went straight to her room, where she relived the last passionate moments she had spent with him. Even in retrospect they set her pulses racing, confirming her realisation that the sooner her charade was over, the better for her emotional safety.

As expected, her sleep was fitful, and seven o'clock found her wandering along the shore, musing on what might have happened had she and Alex spent the entire night on the *Lovely Linda*. So deep was she in thought, she didn't see Kevin until his outstretched arms stopped her.

'Hi, Marly, you don't look your usual cheerful self.'

'With good reason,' she said wryly. 'Our blonde bombshell put paid to the plot I'd set in motion.' As she spoke she remembered she had not yet told him she had deliberately fixed the engine to give trouble, but before she could do so Kevin spoke.

'Fiona was determined not to let you and Alex spend the night together, and when she wants something there's no stopping her.' His voice held reluctant admiration. 'Between you and me, I think she suspected Alex of engineering the whole thing so the engine would give out and he'd have all night to seduce you!'

'He'd have had to be pretty conversant with engines to do that,' she smiled, recollecting his irritability when faced with a mass of plugs and wires.

'He *is* conversant,' Kevin said. 'According to Fiona he races internationally.'

Marly almost danced with rage. The devious, lying swine! From the minute she had suggested taking out the boat he had planned to spend a night with her at sea. Finding the fused cable had been a bonus for him, saving him the trouble of manufacturing a fault. Like her, he had intended making their breakdown appear genuine when they were eventually rescued.

Two minds with but a single thought, she stormed silently, except that he had planned to seduce her, while she had intended to stop on the brink! Which was very odd, for when it came to the crunch he had surprisingly given her an out, and she had surprisingly rejected it.

'Why the war dance?' Kevin enquired.

Taking a couple of deep breaths, she told him, and was entirely unprepared for his shout of laughter.

'Talk about the biter being bit!' he said when he could talk. 'It wouldn't surprise me if Alex *knew* you'd messed with the engine.'

'He could never have guessed that. The fault I created might genuinely have happened, but given his knowledge, he could easily have fixed it.' Humour got the better of her anger, and she smiled ruefully. 'You're right, Kevin. I *was* bit!'

'Not to worry, your secret's safe with me!' Linking his arm companionably through hers, he led her in the direction of the beach house. 'Fiona's a strange girl, you know. Alone with me she's intelligent, but the instant Alex hoves in sight she's like a flighty teenager.'

'But you're still smitten?'

'Unfortunately yes, so all I can do is be around to pick up the pieces.'

'A bit tricky if the pieces fall when she's in England and you're here!'

'I've been offered a job in London when I leave the professor, and I intend taking it.'

Marly hoped he was not storing up more hurt for himself, but long ago she had learned that when it came to love one could not influence another person. All one could do as a friend was to be there when needed, and either congratulate or commiserate.

Although Marly's plan had failed, it was some consolation to know Alex had failed too. Yet he gave no sign of disappointment and continued dividing his attention equally between her and Fiona, making it clear when he was alone with Marly where his real interest lay.

She contrived as many ways as possible to keep him on the boil, while adroitly finding excuses not to go beyond kisses, and by the end of the third day after the boat trip frustration had taken its toll of him, for he appeared on the veranda for breakfast heavy-eyed and grumpy.

'Insomnia,' he said shortly, when she asked if he was unwell.

'I have an excellent cure. When you go to bed, try to recall every single thing you did from the moment you woke up. I promise you'll be out like a light before you reach lunch.'

'I doubt it. Last night, it was thinking of *after* our lunch yesterday that made me sleepless!'

Hot colour washed Marly's cheeks. Yesterday, while Kevin and Fiona had been snorkelling in the bay, Alex had led her to a secluded spot further down the beach and began making love to her. As usual she had responded to his urgency, but as he had edged down the zip of her swimsuit she had come to her senses and pushed him away.

'Alex, don't. This isn't the way to start a relationship,' she had protested.

'Why not? What can be nicer than making love on soft white sand?'

'A soft white bed,' she whispered. 'I want our first time to be perfect, and that means spending the night together and seeing your face on the pillow next to me in the morning.'

Alex had tried to look understanding, but thwarted passion had taxed his patience, and she had realised it was going to be difficult to keep him at arm's length much longer. Because of this she had locked her door that night, worried in case he tried to put her excuse to the test.

'You could at least be more sympathetic.' Alex's disgruntled voice brought her back to the present. 'You've made me wait longer for you than I've waited for any woman.'

Marly's blood boiled. How dared he compare her with his other women? Yet all she said was, 'Expectancy will make it all the nicer.'

'Don't kid yourself. All it does is make it quicker!'

'Don't be cross with me,' she pleaded. 'I've already gone further with you than I should.'

'I'm sorry, Marly. I've no right to take out my frustration on you.'

'You wouldn't need to be frustrated if you . . .' Putting a slight catch in her voice, she played her ace. 'I believe it's important to keep myself pure for my husband, and though I almost gave in to you on the boat, I've come to my senses again. What I'm trying to say is that I won't give myself to a man unless I'm married to him.'

Deliberately she met his eyes. If she had misjudged his feelings for her, or forced the issue too soon, her scheming would come to nothing and she'd have to settle for failure.

For what seemed an age but was probably a few seconds, he was silent, and noting his veiled expression, she thought she had overplayed her hand and lost him. But when he finally spoke, he sounded amused.

'I wasn't aware this was February the twenty-ninth!'

'I beg your pardon?' She pretended ignorance.

'In our society women only propose to men when it's a leap year.'

'You're making a joke of something very serious, Alex. It took courage for me to speak to you so frankly, and just to set the record straight, in our culture too it's usual to wait for the man to do the asking.'

'In that case, when in Rome—or should I say Karon Beach?—I *will* do the asking.' His voice lost its jocular tone and became so deep it was barely audible. 'Will you marry me, Marly?'

Stunned, she gazed at him. Her plan had worked! Yet strangely she felt no sense of triumph. On the contrary, all she felt was depression. Was it because she knew how empty her life was going to be when she finally disclosed her identity and walked out on him?

Yet why assume he had proposed merely to get her into bed, as he had done with Andrea? What if he genuinely wished her to be his wife? The notion was so wonderful that she savoured it.

'I'm waiting for your reply,' Alex said. 'Given that you were the one to propose first, you can't be suffering from shock!'

'I am. I can't believe you mean it.'

'You've left me no option. Marriage was the last thing I had in mind, but I can't see any other way of having you.'

Marly came down to earth with a bump. How cruelly he had knocked off her rose-coloured glasses, showing her how foolish she was to imagine he was anything other than an expedient man out to get what he wanted. As for his proposal, it was obviously as meaningful as the one he had made to Andrea!

But now wasn't the time to laugh in his face. Before she did *that* she would hoist him higher with his own petard, and thus ensure his fall was a very painful one.

She was saved from having to give him his answer by the appearance of Fiona and Kevin, back sooner than she had expected from a game of tennis at the local club.

'Fiona was off-colour,' Kevin explained as he poured himself a glass of fresh papaya juice and took his place at the table.

'I've probably been over-eating,' the girl added, sitting herself beside Alex and resting her hand possessively on his arm. 'Sumalee's such a great cook I can't resist her food.'

For the remainder of the day she stuck to Alex like a leech, which gave Marly the breathing space she needed, and at dinner, which was a barbecue on the beach, she did the same.

As usual Alex held centre stage, proving how knowledgeable he was on a variety of subjects. Like all good talkers he enjoyed debate, and occasionally provoked it simply to cause an argument.

'Take the Amazon rainforests for example,' he said, leaning back against a palm tree and sipping his coffee. 'If the world doesn't stop their wholesale decimation they'll turn into deserts.'

'They're so vast it will take hundreds of years,' Kevin argued.

'We can't just consider ourselves,' Alex replied. 'We have to think of future generations.'

'I agree,' Marly said.

'You agree with everything Alex says,' Fiona complained. 'You're far too docile, Marly.'

Marly was not sure how to reply, and Alex came to her defence.

'Marly is only docile when it suits her,' he commented drily. 'She can be extremely obstinate when the mood takes her.'

Knowing to what he was referring, Marly stared fully into his eyes. 'You make me sound very calculating.'

'Clever,' he corrected. 'You know how to flatter a man and make him feel he's the boss, even if he isn't!'

'Don't most women do the same?'

'Occasionally they try, but I've never encountered anyone as good at it as you!'

'What about me?' Fiona burst out.

'You try,' Alex said, 'but compared with Marly you're an amateur.'

'Thanks!' Fiona exclaimed angrily, and jumping to her feet, stalked off the beach.

'I think she's still off-colour,' Kevin murmured by way of explanation.

'I'll go and see if she's all right,' Marly said, and gratefully seizing the excuse to end the evening, hurriedly followed the younger girl back to the house.

The light was on in Fiona's bedroom, but when Marly tapped on the door, the light went out and a sleepy voice asked who it was.

'Marly. I wondered if I can get you anything?'

'I'm fine, thanks; just tired. I'll see you in the morning.'

As Marly turned to go into her bedroom she stopped in her tracks, startled to see Alex at the end of the short corridor, mouthing her to come towards him and casting a jaundiced eye in the direction of Fiona's door.

Realising he wished to talk to her without the other girl knowing, she had no option but to obey him, and as soon as she was within touching distance his hand came out to clasp hers and draw her outside.

Not pausing on the veranda, he led her down the steps and on to the beach, guiding her across the sand until they were well out of earshot of anyone in the house. Only then did he stop and swing her round to face him. There was a full moon, and in its light she saw the hard set of his mouth and the jut of his jaw, both of which signified tension held in check.

'What's wrong, Marly?' he bit out. 'You've avoided being alone with me since I proposed to you, and I want to know why. If you're going to turn me down I'd like to know why, and if it's yes, then why the hell don't you put me out of my misery?'

The pain in his voice unnerved her, for she had not expected it. Anger yes, even hurt pride because she had not immediately jumped at his offer of marriage, but pain, definitely not.

Could she have misjudged him? Was his offer a genuine one and not the ploy it had been with Andrea? Filled with doubt, she opted for partial truth.

'I had the feeling you proposed to me because I'd pushed you into it.'

'*Pushed* me?'

'You said marriage was the last thing you'd had in mind, but that you couldn't see how else to have me.'

Alex's body went slack with surprise, and Marly took the opportunity of pulling free of his hold and moving away from him.

'It wasn't the most romantic of proposals, Alex. Rawly sexual, yes, but in my view that's no recipe for a lasting relationship.'

'For God's sake, I——'

'No, please let me finish. I know you've avoided marriage, and you've also made it plain you——' She hesitated, trying to use words a well brought-up Thai girl might utilise. 'What I mean is that I know you lust after me, and it's become such a fire inside you that you can't think of anything else except appeasing it. But once you have, you'll tire of me.'

'You think so?' Alex's tone was dry. 'You're wrong, I'm afraid. My fault, of course. I've been a bloody fool and I deserve your censure.'

Marly remained silent, uncertain what was to come yet knowing—given her knowledge of this man—that it would be clever and subtle.

'I *have* avoided marriage until now. No matter how beautiful, charming or intelligent my girlfriends were, I saw no reason to tie myself to one when there was always another who was ready, willing, and able. I'm not saying my behaviour was laudable. I'm merely stating how it was for me. And incidentally, how it is for many men these days. Why have one flower in a vase when an entire bouquet is there for the picking?'

Why indeed? Marly agreed cynically, and thought that women had embraced liberation without weighing up all the pros and cons.

'Then I met *you*,' Alex continued, raking back his hair with his hand, 'and suddenly one flower was all I desired.'

'Only because it wasn't ripe for the picking.'

'That's what *I* thought at first, but the longer I knew you, the more I understood my feelings for you. What began as lust turned into love, and I knew my freedom of choice, which had always been so important to me, was over, because I'd subconsciously made my choice the moment I saw you acting in that silly skit at Christmas. Except that I soon realised you hadn't been acting, for you were as sweet and gentle as the girl you'd been portraying.'

Marly writhed with shame. Innocent she still was, in the biblical sense, but sweet and gentle she wasn't; not with strong-minded older brothers who'd have teased her unmercifully if she hadn't stood up to them. But now was not confession time; there were too many unresolved issues.

'After what you've just told me,' she said carefully, 'I can't fathom why you said what you did when you asked me to marry you.'

'Neither can I!' he said with raw honesty. 'Looking back on it, I suppose I was afraid to let you know how deep my feelings are. I figured that if you assumed it was sexual attraction you would realise the power you have over me.'

'Power?' she echoed.

'To make or break my life.'

His very lack of emphasis lent poignancy to his words, and her doubts dissipated like water in sand. For the second time that day she was filled with joy, and this time it did not vanish. She *would* become Alex's wife.

But first she had to tell him her identity. Even as she went to do so, the memory of Andrea intruded. How would the girl react at learning her friend was going to marry the man who had discarded *her*? Without question she would be hurt, but Marly, now that she had come to know Alex, was certain his proposal to Andrea had been a genuine one, and that not until they had started living together had he realised it had been a mistake. But Andrea was unlikely to see it that way, ego being what it was, and would doubtless be hurt at what she'd regard as Marly's disloyalty.

However, she did owe Andrea an explanation, and until she had spoken to her it didn't seem morally right to give Alex his answer.

'I can't consider your proposal while—er—while Fiona believes she's going to be your wife,' she said in her primmest voice. 'It isn't seemly.'

'Your favourite expression!' Humour creased his face, though it grew serious as he went on, 'Then it looks as if I'll have to return to England with Fiona and break the news when she's in the bosom of the family.'

'Will it be awkward for you?'

'A damn sight less awkward than having to be her husband!' He came a step closer. 'Don't play games with me, Marly.'

'I'm not.' Raising herself on tiptoe, she placed her lips upon his, then drew back and, putting her palms together, lowered her chin to her fingers in a most obeisant *wai*.

'Please stop doing that to me,' he protested.

Knowing she would, once she had managed to speak to Andrea, Marly lowered her chin further still, then with a light laugh ran fleetly across the sand to the house.

CHAPTER THIRTEEN

NEXT day, their last one before returning to Bangkok, Marly still tried to avoid being alone with Alex. She was sorry they weren't returning to Bangkok immediately, instead of tomorrow, for then she could have telephoned Andrea and abandoned her role-playing. What a relief that would be! She was fed up to the teeth with acting the gentle charmer and longed to revert to her normal, sparky self.

But how would Alex react to her real persona? Her docility might have occasionally irritated him, but he had undoubtedly enjoyed feeling he was the one in control. But then what man didn't?

'What are the plans for today?' Kevin questioned as, breakfast over, he perched on the balustrade overlooking the turquoise sea.

'I fancy going to the sports club and getting in some water-skiing,' Alex said.

'Good idea,' the Australian enthused. 'Going to join us, Fiona?'

'No, thanks, I'm for a lazy morning.'

'Still feeling off-colour?'

'Not at all,' she shrugged, and flipped through a pile of magazines on the small table beside her.

Brief shorts and bikini-top drew the eye to the lovely line of her body, and her skin had acquired a deeper tan that accentuated the corn-gold of her silky hair. Despite the violet smudges of tiredness beneath her eyes, she was a truly beautiful girl, and Marly, watching her, was

140

astonished that Alex, with his appreciation of women, had not proved susceptible to her.

'Will *you* join us, Marly?' Alex quizzed.

'Not even if you paid me! I tried it once and thought my arms would be pulled out of their sockets. I'll stay and keep Fiona company.'

'You didn't need to stay behind,' Fiona remarked as the two men drove off in the small runabout that belonged to their host. 'I don't mind my own company.'

'I stayed because I wanted to. We've hardly had a chance to talk to each other.'

'I don't think we've much to say. Unless you want to talk about Alex?'

Marly's heartbeat quickened, though her smile was easy. 'It isn't good policy to discuss the man one is working for.'

'I shouldn't think it good policy to fall in love with him either. Not that I blame you. Most women fall for him but luckily I'm the only one he cares about.'

Marly said nothing and Fiona sat up straighter and stared at her defiantly.

'We *are* getting married, you know. That's why I came out to see him—so we could decide on the date.'

'You've already told me that.'

'But you don't believe me, do you?'

'The question is whether *you* believe you!'

'What's that supposed to mean?'

But Marly felt she had said enough—too much if truth be told—and nervously waited for Fiona to press for an answer. To her relief the girl didn't, and Marly found this psychologically telling, for it showed that she didn't honestly believe in the engagement she was continually parading. Then why did she do it? Was it because she hoped to bludgeon Alex into submission?

'I love Alex,' Fiona said into the silence, her eyes shimmering with tears. 'He means everything to me. No matter how busy he was he always had time for me, even when I was a child. His kindness and silly teasing helped me face the unbearable.'

'I know,' Marly sympathised, and looking into the flushed face appreciated why he had found it difficult to end her dream. But it was a nettle he had to grasp, and the sooner the better. Pushing back her chair, she rose. 'I'm for a swim. It's the only way to cool off.'

Not waiting to see if Fiona would join her, she padded down to the water's edge and walked along the shoreline for several hundred yards before plunging in. What an ideal spot this was for a honeymoon, she thought as she floated on the buoyant waves, and envisaged herself and Alex alone here.

What would he be like as a lover? Passionate, certainly, but it would be tempered with gentleness if his kisses were anything to go by. Still, the pundits said you never knew what a person was like as a lover until you *were* their lover. Of course she could always ask Andrea. The shock of the thought—it had come unbidden into her consciousness—caused her to sink beneath the water, and, spluttering and gasping for breath, she surfaced and made for the beach.

But the thought could not be left behind, and an image of Andrea and Alex lying next to one another, naked and in abandonment, filled her mind's eye, engulfing her in pain. Grow up, she chided herself, sinking on to the sand. You didn't expect him to be a virgin, did you? He must have made love to innumerable women so why get uptight about one in particular? It isn't logical.

Yet logic had little to do with emotion, and the pain remained with her. If only it hadn't been Andrea. Any of her other friends wouldn't have mattered so much, but Andrea was close to her, second only to Nan, and it was agonising to think the same hands that would be caressing her breasts had caressed Andrea's, that the

sensual mouth which had plundered hers had driven deep
into the mouth of a girl with whom she had shared all
her hopes and dreams. With a moan she buried her head
in her hands, willing herself to be adult, to see that the
past was past, and that only the present and the future
counted.

After several moments of soul-searching, Marly raised
her head and breathed deep of the sea-breeze air.
Jealousy had been overcome if not obliterated, and she
was confident that given time this too would happen.
But she did not see Andrea ever being part of her life
again. Nor would her friend want it. It was a sad thought
and it lay heavy on her heart as she rose and returned
to Fiona, who was still lying on a sunbed on the veranda.

A plate of mangoes and papayas, peeled and cut into
the shape of flowers, which was something the Thais
excelled at, had been set on the table, and Marly helped
herself to a fruit.

'Care for one?' she asked.

'No, thanks. I felt ill again in the night so I'm giving
my tummy a rest.'

'Why not let Kevin take a look at you?'

'It isn't necessary. I just ate too much. In fact I think
I'll tell Sumalee to count me out for lunch.'

'I'll do it. I want to go in and shower anyway.'

Marly gave the housekeeper the message, then went
to her room. She had a shower and was drying herself
when she heard Alex talking on the telephone in the
living-room. He was checking something with his secretary, and at the sound of his crisp voice she experienced such an urge to see him that she almost tiptoed
out to beckon him into her room. No need to wonder
what would happen if she did! Suffice it to say Fiona
would have hysterics. Smiling at the thought, she
dropped the towel and slipped into shorts and top.

Kevin and Fiona were in the living-room with Alex when Marly joined them.

'We're going out in the boat,' Kevin informed her. 'I haven't been on it yet and Alex is taking us round some of the islands.'

'I hope we won't have any more engine trouble,' she answered with a straight face, and swung round to the tall, tawny-haired man who had come to stand beside her. 'You should have some lessons in boat maintenance, Alex.'

'You have to be kidding!' Fiona giggled before he could reply. 'There's *nothing* he doesn't know about boats.'

Marly raised wide-apart brown eyes in his direction. 'Really? Then how is it we were marooned the other night?'

'One of those freak happenings,' he replied, meeting her gaze without so much as a blink. 'Even an expert can be flummoxed.' He moved to the door. 'I suggest we get moving. Sumalee's prepared us a picnic and we can have lunch on board.'

They set off in high spirits, as befitted the cloudless blue sky, golden sunshine, and azure sea glinting pure and clear as crystal. If there was pollution in their waters there were no visible signs of it.

Within half an hour Phuket was a smudge on the horizon, and they lolled on deck eating stuffed chicken wings, spicy tiger prawns—large and pink—and tiny ears of corn, marble-size aubergines, and bowls of cardamon-scented rice.

Fiona merely picked at her food, and later was content to lounge on deck while everyone else went swimming, giving the excuse that the Bucks Fizz Alex had served at lunch had made her sleepy. But Marly suspected she was feeling far from well and was putting on a brave face so as not to spoil their day.

It was dusk when they finally returned to the house, and Alex announced that he didn't know about anyone else but he intended having a couple of hours' sleep.

'Me too.' Fiona leaned tiredly against his side. 'Will we be dining in or out?'

'I've booked a table at the yacht club. As it's our last night I thought you two girls would welcome a chance to dress up.'

'What a super idea. I bought a black dress in Paris that will knock you out!'

'You'd be a knock-out in a sack,' Kevin said.

'Which doesn't say much for your fashion sense!'

'Maybe not. But it says a helluva lot for your figure!'

Fiona had to laugh, though the look she cast Alex was faintly aggrieved. 'Why don't *you* ever compliment me? You're always so serious.'

'It's my age,' he retorted. 'I'm what's known as the older generation.'

'Don't be silly. You're in the prime of life.'

'I'm years older than you, my dear. It may not be apparent now, but you'd notice the gap ten years from now. You'll still want to go out dancing while I'll be happy to sit and read by the fire.'

'Rubbish.' Fiona punched him playfully on the arm. 'You're the most active, energetic man I've met, and you'll be the same when you're sixty—just like your father.'

Marly heard Alex's faint sigh and knew exactly how he felt. He could go on talking in this vein till the cows came home and it still wouldn't persuade Fiona they were wrong for one another. Only the brutal truth would do that. Echoing his sigh, she quickened her pace, unwilling to listen to any more of the conversation.

Later that evening, bathed and dressed, she surveyed herself in the mirror and wished she was wearing one of her own dresses instead of Nan's. Not that the pink silk cheong-sam wasn't beautiful; it was, but it was at variance with her own style, which her friends called high fashion, and her mother referred to as gimmicky!

Still, if she managed to contact Andrea tomorrow she could confront Alex in the evening as herself—providing they managed to sneak time together without Fiona finding out. Marly frowned, wondering when the girl was returning to England and whether he'd be flying back with her.

Picking up her hairbrush, she brushed her glossy black hair. It fell like a velvet cloud to her shoulders, enhancing her air of fragility, but again it was a false picture of her, for she was a strong girl with a forceful personality. Again she wondered if Alex would be dismayed by this, and could not quell a *frisson* of anxiety.

As she came on to the terrace, she saw him standing by the wooden railing, staring out at the moonlit ocean. At her step he turned and came towards her, impeccably dressed in white trousers and black crocodile Gucci belt, with a thin, black cotton open-necked sports shirt, the sleeves rolled up to reveal bronzed, muscular arms.

'Do you know this is the first time we've been alone today?' he said deeply.

Before she could answer, Kevin appeared in the doorway. 'I think we should get Fiona to a hospital.'

'Why? What's wrong?' Alex demanded.

'She has violent stomach pains and I think it's appendicitis.'

Alex strode swiftly into Fiona's room, where she was lying on the bed, her face pale and glistening with sweat.

'Sorry to be such a nuisance.' She smiled wanly. 'I'm sure Kevin's fussing over nothing.'

'I'm sure he isn't,' Alex replied bluntly, leaning forward to clasp her hand. 'He's a doctor, sweetie, and they don't make a fuss without reason.'

'I still think I can hang on until we get back to Bangkok.'

Alex glanced at Kevin. 'What do you think?'

'She should be in hospital now.'

'In that case there's nothing further to discuss.'

A call to the yacht club ascertained that there was an excellent hospital a few miles away, and within the hour Fiona was installed there and had been seen by a surgeon, who confirmed Kevin's diagnosis and said she should be operated on immediately.

'Can't I fly back to Bangkok and have the operation there?' a tearful Fiona pleaded, holding tightly to Alex's hand. 'You're all going back tomorrow and I'll be left here alone.'

'No, you won't,' he soothed. 'I'll stay with you.'

'You can't. You said you had some architects flying in from Hong Kong and——'

'They'll wait for me. *I'm* the client, my dear, and too valuable a one for them to make a fuss. Now stop worrying.'

Tears rolled down her cheeks. 'You're so good to me, Alex. I'm being a dreadful nuisance, and——'

'You aren't. You'll ill and I want to be with you. It's what brothers are for.'

'You aren't my brother.'

'I feel as if I am,' he said softly, stroking her hair. 'Relax and stop worrying.'

Fiona went to reply but the injection the doctor had given her was already taking effect, and her eyelids drooped shut over eyes already becoming unfocused.

'There's no reason for you to stay with Fiona,' Kevin said to Alex as she was wheeled away and they all retired to the waiting-room. 'I've a few days left of my vacation and I'm more than willing to remain here.'

Marly found her heart beating faster as she waited for Alex to reply. She knew he didn't love the girl, yet he had been so tender with her that jealousy had reared its head again.

'Thanks for the offer, Kevin, but I think it's my duty to stay. Fiona's very dependent on me, and——'

'She'll go on being dependent unless you do something drastic.'

'I intend to. But when she's recovering from an operation is hardly the time.'

'It's the best time,' Kevin argued. 'I know it's none of my business but I think Fiona's problem is she's scared of being left alone—the way she was when her parents died. She became fixated on you, and she can't let go. But if she were forced to transfer her dependency to someone else—which she'd have to do if she were left here with only me to turn to—it might make her realise you aren't the only man she can rely on.'

'I doubt if it will be that simple,' Alex muttered.

'It's worth giving it a try.'

'If it works, I hope you know what you're letting yourself in for?'

'I do.'

The two men looked at each other and came to an unspoken agreement, and Marly, watching them, couldn't help thinking how differently two women would have handled such a situation. Certainly not as quickly, nor with such a lack of *Angst*.

It was well after midnight when they returned to the house, having stopped off for a meal in the coffee-shop of one of the main hotels. Marly was very tired and went straight to bed, but once there found she could not sleep, beset by a nameless anxiety that finally coalesced into the fear that when she told Alex she loved him and disclosed her identity, he would be so furious, he would walk away from her.

After all, he was a proud man, and to discover she had thought so badly of him that she had wanted to pay him back for his behaviour might raise a host of questions in his mind; the most important one being why, once she had got to know him and fallen in love with him, she had not come right out and asked to hear his side of the story.

There was no answer to this, of course. Well, there *was* an answer, but giving it would be like waving a red rag at a bull. How did you tell a man you instinctively sided with a woman when a male-female relationship didn't work out?

'It's been a marvellous few days, Marly,' Alex said gruffly over coffee in the departure lounge, where they sat waiting to fly back to Bangkok. 'But it would have been even better if we'd been on our own.'

'It wouldn't have been possible,' she chastised in her sweetest tone.

'I realise you could never have gone away with me unchaperoned,' he said huskily.

Unable to meet his gaze, she lowered her head. This was getting worse and worse. Perhaps she should tell him the truth now, and not wait until she had spoken to Andrea?

'Alex, there's something I——'

'Alex, my dear! What a wonderful surprise to see you.'

The greeting, in heavily accented English, came from a tall, red-haired, voluptuous beauty in her mid-thirties. She was accompanied by a short, plump man with iron-grey hair, who was at least two decades her senior.

'Inge!' Alex jumped to his feet. 'I'd no idea you were in this part of the world.'

He kissed her on both cheeks, then shook the man's hand before introducing the couple to Marly as Inge and Per Svensson, from Stockholm. He offered them no explanation as to his relationship with Marly, merely saying they had been staying with another couple at a friend's house.

The Swedish couple, who Marly later discovered owned the largest sportswear company in Europe, monopolised Alex throughout the flight, giving her no chance to make her confession. Even when they arrived in Bangkok, the Svenssons remained with them, for they were staying at the Hamilton Hotel, and Alex naturally offered them a lift in the chauffeur-driven car that had come to meet him.

'Any chance of you having dinner with us tonight?' Inge asked as they entered the air-conditioned foyer.

The invitation was echoed by her husband, whose glance, unlike his wife's, included Marly.

'I may be tied up with business,' Alex replied. 'Give me a chance to look through my messages first, and I'll call your room and let you know.'

They parted at the lift, the Svenssons taking the express one to the penthouse floor, and Marly and Alex going to his office on the first floor. As she glanced at him as they walked down the corridor, her heart seemed to turn over in her breast. What a magnificent specimen of a man he was. Unbelievable to think they would be spending the rest of their lives together. But oh, lord, she hadn't yet told him she was going to marry him!

He turned his head and, seeing her watching him, reached for her hand. 'Forgive me, darling,' he whispered.

'For what?'

'I should have dropped you home first. I don't expect you to work today.'

'Why not? I've a mass of things to catch up on. But I'd like to talk to you first.'

'Not until I've kissed you.' They had reached the private entrance to his office and he opened the door and ushered her inside. But as he went to take her in his arms, his latest secretary, Mrs Dewsbury, came through from her office.

'Thank goodness you're here at last, Mr Hamilton!' she greeted him with undisguised relief. 'Your father tried to contact you early this morning in Phuket but you'd already left. He asked for you to call him the instant you arrived.'

'Did he say why?'

'It's to do with the new hotel in Hawaii. Shall I get him on the line for you?'

'Please.'

As he crossed to his desk, Marly went to the door. 'I'll be in my office. Let me know when you're free.'

It was lunchtime when Mrs Dewsbury called and asked her to go to Alex's office, and anticipating a meal with him, she was dismayed to find him standing by his desk, stuffing files into his briefcase. His grey suit and dark tie made it unnecessary for him to tell her he was leaving the country, and she bit back a sigh in the knowledge that she would have to maintain her role until his return.

'Sorry about this, Marly.'

'How long will you be away?'

'I won't know till I get to London.'

'I thought you were going to Hawaii?'

'Afterwards. I'll be in London a week.' He frowned as he consulted a piece of paper in his hand on which she could see several sets of figures.

'It sounds as if you'll be gone some time.'

'I——' He broke off as his intercom buzzed and Mrs Dewsbury reminded him that his car was waiting, and he was cutting it fine.

With a muttered imprecation he picked up his briefcase and strode to the door. Expecting him to stop and draw her into his arms, Marly was confounded when he only gave her a brief kiss and an even briefer smile.

'Looks as if we're out of sync with each other, Marly. It will have to be another time, another place.'

She was still standing there, bemused, when the door closed behind him and she was alone. For an instant she thought she was going to burst into tears, then common sense reasserted itself and she drew a deep breath. Alex was clearly concerned with the situation in Hawaii and could not think of anything else. Heavens, she had been working long enough to know the truth of the old adage that for a man love was a thing apart, though it was a woman's whole existence. Well, perhaps it wasn't quite so true these days, but it was still true enough for it to have validity.

'You don't look as if you've come back from a holiday on paradise island!' Nan greeted her when she walked into the house later that afternoon.

Forcing a smile, Marly carried her case to her bedroom, with Nan in tow. 'Phuket was exactly the paradise you described.'

'Then what's with the long face? No, let me guess. Trouble with Alex Hamilton.'

Marly turned from hanging away the cheong-sams she had taken with her. 'In a way. He asked me to marry him.'

Nan's mouth fell open. 'You said no, of course?'

Marly shook her head, then added, 'But I haven't yet said yes either.'

'Is this a magical mystery tour or are you going to explain?'

'I do love him, I have for quite a while but I refused to admit it because of Andrea. That's why I won't say yes to him until I've spoken to her.'

'I don't envy you having to tell her.'

'I'm dreading it,' Marly admitted. 'I want to get it over as soon as I can.'

'Then call her now. It's eight in the morning British time and she won't have left for her office. If she's terribly upset, it might help if I have a word with her too.'

Flinging Nan a grateful look, Marly dialled Andrea's number. Her hand was shaking and she had to do it twice, but eventually she heard the ringing tone.

'There's no answer,' she said when it had rung for more than a minute. 'She may be out of town. I'll call her office later.'

'You won't want to talk to her there!'

'Obviously. But I can find out from the switchboard if she *is* away. Having to keep dialling would put me on tenterhooks each time.'

'Poor love.' Nan came over and gave her a hug. 'Let's go out for a meal and you can tell me how Kevin got on with Fiona.'

'I'd forgotten all about her! She had her appendix out last night and he stayed behind to be with her.' Marly rummaged in her bag for the number of the clinic. 'I must see how she is.'

'Feeling sorry for herself,' Kevin explained, coming on the line when the call was put through to Fiona's room. 'She was allergic to the pain-killer they gave her, though she's not so nauseous now. I'll give her your love.'

'Do that. I just hope she gives hers to *you*!'

Marly felt less fraught after she had talked to Kevin, for it brought home to her that one couldn't account for love—either for falling in or falling out of it. If only she could make Andrea see this too. If she couldn't, they probably wouldn't speak to each other again.

CHAPTER FOURTEEN

CONTACTING Andrea proved easier said than done, for her office said she had taken a few days' leave, and as far as they were aware was spending it at home. But though Marly telephoned early in the morning and late at night, she was still unable to contact her.

As if that weren't bad enough, there was no word from Alex either, and though she told herself he was probably inundated with problems, deep down she was surprised that no matter how busy he was he had not found a spare moment to call her. Inevitably, doubts began to disturb her. Was out of sight out of mind? Had his offer of marriage merely been a means to an end—like his proposal to Andrea—and did he now feel differently?

Finally, nearly a week after his departure, she and Nan were watching a video in her room when she did receive a call from London. But it was from Andrea, not Alex.

'Where on earth have you been?' Marly asked after the usual greetings. 'I've been trying to reach you for ages.'

'So I gather from the office. But this isn't simply a return call. I'd have phoned anyway. Something fantastic has happened.'

Marly caught her breath. How wonderful if Andrea had fallen in love again. 'Tell me,' she said quickly.

'I'm getting married tomorrow.'

'That's marvellous. I'm so happy for you.' And happy for myself, she nearly added, for now her friend had a new man in her life she would find it easier to forgive Marly for marrying the old one. 'Who is he?'

'Alex, of course. Who else?'

Marly began to shake and the telephone wobbled so precariously in her hand that she set it on the table. Seeing it, Nan jumped up and came over to her.

'What is it?' she whispered.

'Alex has gone back to Andrea.'

'You're joking!'

Marly shook her head, totally incapable of speaking. Yet she had to say something, for she could hear Andrea's voice coming through the receiver, faint but persistent.

'Marly, I can't hear you. Are you there?'

Lifting the receiver, Marly spoke. 'Y-yes. The line went dead for a minute.'

'Sorry. I was saying that apart from my immediate family you're the first to know. Alex arrived in London several days ago and came to see me. He said he'd made a terrible mistake breaking our engagement and begged me to forgive him. I tried to keep him dangling for a bit, but he was so distraught I didn't have the heart. He's a changed man, Marly.'

'I'm glad to hear it.' To her own ears Marly's voice sounded faint, but Andrea was too full of happiness to take in anything else.

'And guess what?' she babbled on. 'We're honeymooning in Hawaii! Can you imagine anything more romantic? He has to go there on business so he thought we should rush the wedding and combine the two.'

Marly collapsed on to a chair. Alex's perfidy was like a knife in her gut and she doubled up with the pain of it. Knowing him as she did, she was certain that his decision had not been a sudden one, which meant that even while he had been pursuing *her* he had resolved to marry Andrea. The doubts she had felt about him these last few days had proved correct. His proposal had merely been a ruse to get her into bed, and had he not been called away he would have succeeded.

'Marly, are you still there?' Andrea called.

'Sorry. I was just digesting your news. Are you sure you're doing the sensible thing? I mean, he let you down once and he can do it again.'

'No way. He's a changed character.'

Marly nearly threw up, and it took all her will-power not to tell Andrea she was making a big mistake.

'He never went off to another woman, you know, which was what I thought,' her friend continued. 'He just wasn't certain he was ready for the commitment of marriage. But now he is and, well, you know what they say about a reformed rake!'

'That they remain a rake,' Marly burst out before she could stop herself.

Andrea laughed, thinking the comment to be a joke. 'I wish you and Nan could be here for my wedding, but it's all rushed because of his Hawaii trip and we're just having a family lunch and waiting till we return to London before having a proper reception. Do you think you'll be home by then?'

'I'm not sure,' Marly hedged, certain that dancing at Alex's wedding was the last thing she would want to do.

'Is Nan there?' Andrea asked. 'I'd like to talk to her.'

'She's out,' Marly lied, seeing Nan shake her head vigorously.

'I'll leave you to tell her my news, then.'

'Have you told Alex you have a friend working at his hotel?' Marly couldn't help asking.

'No—and I don't intend telling him either. We may be coming to Bangkok from Hawaii, and I'd like it to be a surprise.'

It certainly will be, Marly thought grimly. 'When do you think you'll be here?'

'Well, Alex says it may be three weeks before he clears the problems at the Hawaii Hamilton, but you can put the champagne on ice any time after that, I suppose!'

'Will do,' Marly said, and was thankful when the call ended and she could collapse on the bed.

'Calling Alex a swine is an insult to a pig,' Nan commented sombrely. 'He deserves to be boiled in oil for the way he led you on!'

'I'd settle for a shot through the heart, if he had one!' Marly said as she dabbed at her eyes.

'Why didn't you put Andrea wise?'

'I was tempted, but I thought it might sound like jealousy. Anyway, she's not a fool, and I'm sure she's considered the pitfalls.'

'She sounded as if she hadn't considered *anything*,' Nan expostulated. 'With his charisma, Alex can pull the wool over the keenest eyes.' The telephone rang and she leaned across the bed to answer it. It's *him*! she mouthed, disbelief on her face.

Marly jack-knifed off the bed and darted to the far side of the room, almost as though he could see her. 'I can't talk to him,' she whispered in a strangled voice. 'What can he have to say?'

'That he adores you?' Turning her mouth to the receiver, Nan spoke into it. 'I'm sorry, Mr Hamilton, but Marly's gone to stay with friends in Chiang Mai.'

'Damn!' His voice was loud and clear. 'I won't be able to call her until I'm in Hawaii. Will you tell her that?'

'Yes.' Nan almost choked on the word.

'Another thing; would you——?'

The rest of his words were lost, for Nan quietly put down the receiver. 'I couldn't bear to listen to him a moment longer,' she explained. 'He must be mad to think you'd want to speak to him after what he's done.'

'He doesn't realise I know. He has no idea I'm a friend of Andrea's.'

'I'd forgotten that! When will you tell him?'

'Never. If I'd finished programing the software I'd leave Bangkok tomorrow.' Marly ran slender fingers through her silky hair, pushing it away from her face. 'I can't be around when he returns from Hawaii. I can't!'

'I'll take a bet with you he won't bring Andrea here. He'll find some excuse for sending her back to England so he can continue his seduction of *you*.'

'Don't!' Marly shuddered.

'Sorry. I was just trying to warn you. Anyway, I can't keep saying you aren't here every time he calls.'

'Yes, you can. And so can the switchboard at the hotel. I'll talk to them.'

It was a good thing she did, for true to his word, Alex tried to contact her the day he arrived in Hawaii, and kept calling twice a day until Marly told the hotel, as well as Nan, to say she had gone on holiday and had not given them a return date.

Two weeks after her conversation with Andrea, by dint of working all hours she had completed the bulk of the software programing, and called her boss in London to say she was returning home and would finalise it there.

'You surprise me,' he commented. 'I thought you'd be keen to stay in Bangkok as long as possible. I hear it's a great city and that the hotel is sensational.'

'Both are, but I'm homesick. I'll be catching the next available flight home.'

She was fortunate enough to obtain a seat on a plane for the next day. It meant changing at Frankfurt for a connection to London, but her determination to leave before Alex's return was so strong, it was worth the inconvenience.

She was zipping up the last of her cases in her bedroom on the afternoon of her departure, when Nan burst in, hastily shutting the door behind her.

'Alex is here!'

A pile of clothes fell from Marly's nerveless hands. 'I don't believe it!'

'Believe it; and the mood he's in, he'll come storming up here if you don't go down to him!'

'How can he have the gall to try to see me?'

'Easily. He doesn't realise that you know he's married, and he can't fathom why you won't accept his calls.'

'I absolutely won't see him.'

'You must. This is show-down time, remember?'

So it was! Marly caught her breath. At last she could hit Alex where it would hurt him the most—on his ego! How could she have forgotten her plan to cut him down to size when it was the one reason she had embarked on her charade?

'You're right,' she said, and with trembling hands smoothed her hair. As she did, she realised she was wearing her own clothes, not Nan's, and glanced quickly into the mirror opposite her. She was the epitome of a successful business executive in a navy pin-striped viscose and silk trouser suit, the jacket cut with military precision, though the white silk blouse beneath it was softened by a small bow at her throat. It was a far cry from the ultra-feminine outfits Alex had seen her in, and he would be astonished if he saw her like this. Yet how better to let him know that the Marly he had asked to marry him was as much a charade as his declaration of love had been?

Firmly she reached for the loose, flowing caftan that lay on the bed, and slipped it on. An experienced traveller, she always wore something easy-fitting during a long flight, and the caftan was going into her hand luggage, ready for her to change into once she was airborne.

'Why are you wearing that now?' Nan asked, puzzled.

'To make my confession even more exciting,' Marly replied, and high heels clicking on the marble floor, went down to the living-room.

Alex was standing by the window. He was dark-suited, his pristine-white shirt threw his tanned face into relief, and though his mouth curved in a smile as he strode towards her, his eyes were the grey of storm clouds, betokening suppressed anger.

'Hello, Alex,' she smiled. 'You're back earlier than I expected.'

'I'm only staying overnight; then I have to return to Hawaii.'

'You're just here for a day?'

'I came to see *you*.'

She gaped at him. What sort of a monster had poor Andrea married?

'Why the amazement?' he went on. 'You wouldn't accept my calls and I had to find out why.'

'My work was falling behind schedule and I decided not to take *any* calls,' she replied evenly.

It was Alex's turn to gape. 'You wouldn't speak to me because of your damn work? But I'm the man you love, for God's sake!'

'I never said so.'

'Not in words, perhaps, but the way you acted I——'

'That's all it was,' she cut in, seizing the opening he had given her. 'An act.'

He frowned in puzzlement. 'I don't follow.'

'Maybe this will help.'

With a flourish she slipped off her caftan, and Alex's gaze fastened on her clothes. His brows drew together in a frown which slowly dissolved into incredulity, and he shook his head as if unable to absorb what he was seeing.

'Why did you do it?' he finally asked.

'For fun.' Marly managed to twist her lips into a smile. 'When you assumed I was Thai, after the staff Christmas revue, I thought it would be amusing to see how long I could fool you. I was positive you'd soon guess the truth, and when you didn't I got carried away by the whole thing. Of course when you asked me to marry you, I had a fit. I mean, I didn't think you were serious about me, and——'

'I wasn't,' he intervened smoothly, and unexpectedly chuckled. 'Looks as though we've both been had, Marly. That *is* your name, I assume?'

She nodded, not bothering to say it was short for Amalia.

'I fancied you like crazy,' he went on, 'but your virginal act fooled me, and I believed that the only way of having you was to—er——'

'Don't get tongue-tied over it, Alex. I was well aware that your offer of marriage was a ploy. That's why I stalled with my answer.'

'You played me for a real fool, didn't you?'

'You did the same to me!'

'True.' The frown returned. 'How come you speak the language so fluently?'

'My great-grandmother was Thai, and I suppose it gave me an affinity with the tongue.'

Hands in the pockets of his trousers, a typically masculine stance that heightened her awareness of his muscled thighs, he rocked back on his feet as he regarded her, and though she returned his stare coolly, she was memorising every detail of him: his thick, tawny hair, the cleft in his firm chin, the sensual mouth that had sucked and teased and almost tempted her into submission. From today she would never see him, but his image would forever remain with her; a haunting reminder of the might-have-been.

'You can't blame me for wanting you, Marly,' he murmured.

'I don't blame you, Alex. I just don't like you very much.'

'I don't see why. I'm not angry with *you*.'

'You behaved far worse than I did, Alex,' she replied. 'You believed I was an innocent girl, yet you didn't have a twinge of conscience about lying to get me into bed.'

'I didn't think of it in those terms. I wanted you, and I was pretty sure all it required was a little persuasion.'

'Little!' Marly almost exploded. 'If you regard a phoney marriage proposal as a "little persuasion", what would you do if you wanted to exert a *big* influence on someone? Murder them?'

He grinned. 'You know what I mean, Marly. You were passionate and responsive, and——'

'You'd have been up the creek if I'd said yes. Or would you have had your way with me,' she went on in mock Gothic tones, 'and then said the whole thing was a terrible mistake?'

A wave of colour stained his cheekbones and she revelled in his shame and dug in the knife deeper. 'I suppose it's something you've done before?'

He half turned away. 'Let's say it's something I won't be repeating.'

'Which makes my sacrifice worthwhile.'

'Sacrifice?'

'You don't think it was easy pretending you'd bowled me over? You're a gorgeous hunk of man, as I'm sure many women have told you, but you don't have the spark to light me up.'

'Pity,' he drawled. 'Now I know you're a liberated lady, I think we'd be even better together!'

'Sorry, no can do.' Did she sound as matter-of-fact as she thought she did? If so, she was giving a gold medal performance. 'I'm sorry you flew from Hawaii for nothing.'

'No big deal. As the saying goes, you win some, you lose some.'

Feeling as though she had been stabbed, Marly lowered her eyes to her watch. 'I'm sorry I can't offer you a drink, but I'm in an awful rush. I have to be at the airport in an hour.'

'Where are you going?'

'To England. The bulk of my work is finished, and I can finalise it in London. It's more cost-effective for you.'

'I've never quibbled over the cost, and I think you'd do a better job if you remained here till you completed the software.'

'It isn't necessary. Anyway, I can't. I have another job lined up for me.'

'I hope it isn't in Sweden. You'd have a tough task pretending to be a tall ash-blonde!'

'I wouldn't even try! You've witnessed my first and last acting performance!' She cast another glance at her watch and he took the hint and went to the door.

'Goodbye, Marly. Maybe we'll meet again one day.'

Not if I can help it, she thought, and silently watched him walk through the compound to where his car was parked outside the gates. Thank goodness she hadn't lost her temper with him, or worse still, let him see the depth of her hurt. Eventually she would stop loving him, but it was going to be a long, painful haul.

Very long. Very painful.

CHAPTER FIFTEEN

'A LETTER for you, Marly,' Jenny Hunter, one of her flatmates, said.

Seeing it was from Nan, she excitedly tore it open. 'Wonderful news! Kevin and Fiona are engaged.'

'So your matchmaking worked.'

'It took a while. I've been back over two months.'

'Not everyone falls in love at first sight, like you,' the other girl remarked drily, Marly having confided the whole story to her on her return from Bangkok.

Jenny worked for the same company as Marly, and over the past two years they had become firm friends. They shared a three-bedroom apartment in one of the finest developments in Docklands with Jenny's boyfriend Tony Parker, for it was the only way they could afford the mortgage on such expensive accommodation.

'Any news of Alex?' Jenny went on.

'Not from Nan. He's no longer running the Bangkok Hamilton, and I only hear of him from Andrea.'

Indeed her friend's letters from Hawaii were ecstatic. Alex was proving to be an ideal husband, and though Marly was delighted to hear it, the glowing descriptions Andrea gave of her new life filled Marly with such pain that it dashed any hope she had of quickly getting over him. For this reason she replied to each long letter with a brief card, hoping it would eventually cause Andrea's outpourings to cease.

Staring at her computer screen later in the day, Marly accepted that if she didn't pull herself together she would become sour and embittered, thinking of what might have been instead of concentrating on what could be.

'Penny for your thoughts.'

Looking up, she saw Gordon Murray, the managing director of the furniture company for whom she was devising a software program, standing by her desk.

'They're not even worth half of that,' she smiled, thinking he had the kindest blue eyes and the thickest brown hair she had ever seen. And if he didn't fancy her like mad, he was certainly giving an excellent imitation of it!

'You wouldn't be free to have dinner with me tomorrow night?' he asked.

'I would, and I will!' she replied promptly. She had spent an enjoyable evening with him a week ago, so why not again? Gordon, if not as handsome and charismatic as Alex, came a good second. 'What time will you call for me?'

'Eight?'

'Perfect.'

He took her to an Italian restaurant in the King's Road. It had recently opened to high acclaim and consequently was packed.

'I hope it's as good as it's reputed to be,' she commented as they were shown to their table.

'If it isn't, *you* look good enough to eat.'

She grinned, pushing her hair away from her face. 'Not better than the pasta they serve. It's supposed to be like Mamma used to make!'

'Not my Mamma!' he assured her. 'Haggis was her speciality!'

'That's one thing I've never tasted.'

'Each time I go home to Edinburgh she gives me one to put in the freezer. Have dinner at my flat one night, and I'll serve it to you.'

Why not? Marly mused. She was under no illusion he had more than serving haggis in mind, and let him know in as many words that she didn't hop into bed after a few pleasant dates.

'I never thought you did,' Gordon answered, frowning. 'And that's a plus in my book. I'm very attracted to you, Marly, as I'm sure you know, but I'm willing to wait until you feel ready.'

Fine words, she mused, but how would he feel if he knew it might be a very long wait? She gave a deep sigh, not knowing where it came from nor how to hold it back.

'Care to tell me what's troubling you?' he encouraged sympathetically. 'I don't have to be a mind-reader to guess you're trying to get over someone.'

'You're right, but I'd rather not discuss it.'

'If ever you do, I'm something of an expert on broken hearts, and I'll be happy to help mend yours!'

Marly half smiled. 'You could be on a hiding to nothing.'

'I happen to think you're a risk worth taking.' He raised his glass of wine to hers. 'To friends and—I hope—lovers!'

When he kissed her goodnight outside her front door, she did her best to respond, and though she had to feign it, it had nothing to do with his expertise. His touch was confident, his hands light but knowing how to arouse, yet all she could think of was Alex's hands, Alex's mouth, Alex's body.

But it's early days yet, she consoled herself as she undressed and slipped under the duvet. As long as Gordon remained content not to rush her, he might, given time, turn out to be, if not the man of her dreams, a very good substitute.

The consolation she gained from this notion was brief, for it was dramatically shattered the following evening. Jenny was at a business seminar and would not be home till late, and she and Tony, comfortable in tracksuits and slippers, were watching television in the living-room when the doorbell rang.

As Marly was nearest the door, she went to open it and, stupefied, saw the unmistakable figure of Alex. The blood drained from her head and she felt she was going to faint.

'Wh-what are you doing here?'

'Not selling encyclopaedias!' he growled. 'What do you think I'm doing? I've come to see you.'

'You must be insane!'

'Over *you*.' He rattled the door-chain. 'This doesn't feel particularly strong and I'm prepared to break it, so be sensible and let me in.'

'No. I've nothing to say to you.'

'I've plenty for both of us.' He caught hold of the chain. 'Well?'

The roughness in his voice brooked no denial, and short of having a slanging match on the front doorstep she had to do as he asked. With trembling fingers she undid the chain and stepped aside to let him enter.

In the bright light of the hall she noticed for the first time how haggard he was. Deeply etched lines were carved down either side of his nose and there were dark shadows beneath his eyes. His skin too had lost its glow, and despite its usual tan appeared sallow. It was as if he had been ill and had not fully recovered. Her heart lurched and she quickly averted her gaze. If this was what a happy marriage had done, heaven help him if he ever contemplated divorce!

'You're more beautiful than ever,' he stated flatly. 'I haven't been able to forget you and I had to see you again. I—— ' He broke off as they entered the sitting-room and he saw Tony sprawled on the sofa.

Stiltedly she introduced them. 'Tony Parker, Alex Hamilton. Alex is the man I worked for in Bangkok.'

'A great place to live,' Tony said genially.

'Yes.' Alex stood rigid as a post. 'Forgive me for barging in. I didn't realise——'

'Don't worry about interrupting the programme.' Misunderstanding, Tony flicked off the television and rose. 'I can watch the rest of the play in the bedroom. I dare say you and Marly have things to talk over.'

He sauntered out and Alex swung round to Marly, his grey eyes steely, his mouth a hard line. 'He's a cool customer. In the same circumstances I'd be damned if I'd leave you alone.'

Instantly she knew he had misinterpreted the situation, and gratefully seized on it to end a meeting which was causing her unbearable anguish. How *could* Alex be so two-faced? Knowing Andrea was married to him filled her with such nausea that she had to turn away.

'How long has your friend been living here?' Alex questioned into the silence.

Marly drew a deep breath. 'Two years. We bought the flat together.' It was no lie, though she was guilty of the sin of omission, having not mentioned Jenny, who was a third partner in the purchase.

'So you were living with him when you embarked on your charade with me?' Alex went on.

'Yes.'

'Dammit! Have you no shame? The way you led me on, the things you said and——'

'It was an act,' she cut in. 'Where's your sense of humour?'

'Drowned in the waters off Phuket,' he said heavily. 'Do you ever think of that night on the boat, Marly, when you lay in my arms? If the coastguards hadn't appeared you'd have given yourself to me. I take it your boyfriend doesn't know *that*?'

'Shall I ask him to come in so you can tell him?'

'God! You're a cool customer.'

'So are you.'

She clenched her hands tightly, her nails digging so hard into her palms that she knew she would bear the marks for days. She longed to scream Andrea's name, to tell him she knew he was married and that his wife was her close friend. Yet if she let her anger erupt, her love for him might erupt with it, and Alex, being the vile and clever man he was, would realise that if he continued laying siege to her she might eventually succumb to him.

'Are you going to marry Tony Parker?'

'What?' Deafened by her thoughts, Marly stared at him uncomprehendingly.

'Are you going to marry him?'

'It's none of your business.'

'You're right. It isn't. I shouldn't have come here. You were right about that too.' Brushing past her, he went into the hall. 'We don't have anything to say to each other. Goodbye, Marly, I wish you the luck you deserve.'

She heard the front door open and close, but even then she was incapable of moving. Damn him for coming back into her life! For showing her she wanted him as much as ever; that she loved him as much as ever; and that any hope of forgetting him was as much a dream as ever.

Marly was not surprised to hear from Andrea next morning. Since Alex's visit she had surmised that her friend was in London and would be in touch with her.

'You're a lousy correspondent,' Andrea complained. 'It's lucky for our friendship that I'll be staying here for the next year!'

It was bad news for Marly though she managed to hide it. 'I've been meaning to send you a newsy letter but life's been absolutely hectic.'

'Anyone special?'

'Why should it be a man? Maybe it's my work!'

'Phooey! Who is he?'

'Someone for whom I'm currently working. But it's early days yet. Let's get back to you. When did you arrive?'

'Late yesterday afternoon.'

Marly trembled. Alex certainly hadn't wasted time coming to see her. Whatever reason he had given his unsuspecting wife, one thing was indisputable: it hadn't been the truth!

'When can we see you?' Andrea demanded. 'I'm dying for you to meet Alex.'

'I'm terribly busy at the moment and——'

'Too busy to meet your best friend's husband?' came the incredulous screech. 'What's wrong, Marly? Are you ill or something?'

At the concern in Andrea's voice, Marly knew she had no choice. 'I'm fine. But I've been working like a demon and I'm exhausted and look a mess. Won't next week——?'

'Absolutely not. I want to see you this evening. If you have a date, bring him along too.'

'I don't have a date.'

'Then come straight from work and we can chew the fat before Alex arrives. He's tied up with meetings till eight.' Andrea's voice held laughter. 'I can't wait for him to meet you. When he discovers that the girl who created such a brilliant software program for Hamilton Hotels is my closest friend, he'll be astonished.'

He certainly will, Marly thought, and not least because he'll be dead scared I might tell you he also asked *me* to marry him!

At seven that evening, Marly found herself laughing and crying as she hugged the tall, slim, radiant blonde in the multi-coloured Lacroix two-piece.

'You look like a million dollars!' she exclaimed.

'Not quite as expensive as that,' Andrea giggled. 'My loving bridegroom took me shopping in Paris on our way here.' She held Marly at arm's length and examined her. 'You look pretty fantastic yourself. What's this nonsense about looking a mess?'

Not waiting for a reply, she pulled Marly into the vast living-room, where sliding glass doors framed a flower-filled terrace affording a bird's-eye view of Hyde Park and Knightsbridge. Gesturing her to sit on one of the cream suede sofas, Andrea filled two glasses with champagne and handed her one.

'To happy marriages,' she toasted. 'May the next one be yours!'

Marly drank deeply, hoping the champagne would lessen the deep depression that weighed on her like a leaden shroud. Yet it grew heavier as she listened to her friend extol the virtues of her husband, who was not only the most loving and passionate man in the world, but also the kindest and tenderest.

'I remember how cynical you were about rakes reforming,' she concluded, 'but the other night Alex said the idea of returning to the life he led before he met me gives him nightmares.'

'I'm glad I was wrong,' Marly ground out, marvelling that the anguish inside her wasn't outwardly visible. But painstakingly applied cosmetics and an emerald silk wisp of a dress were sufficiently eye-catching to draw attention away from the haunted look in her eyes.

'Now tell me what's been happening to *you*,' Andrea requested.

Seeing it as a way of stopping further tales of how wonderful Alex was, Marly launched into a fictitious account of the socially exciting life she was leading. She had exhausted the topic of Gordon and two invented boyfriends, when she heard the door of the vestibule slam shut. Alex had arrived! Her mouth went dry and

she could not utter a word. Not that Andrea noticed,
for she had jumped to her feet and was already half out
of the room.

'Darling!' she cried. 'I've missed you.'

Marly didn't hear the reply, but a faint sound made
it plain that a passionate embrace was ensuing. On trembling legs she rose and went to stand by the window;
anything to help keep her distance from Alex. Blindly
she stared through the glass, praying for the courage to
carry off the meeting without dissolving into tears.

'Alex, I want you to meet the girl who created what
you said was a brilliant software package for your
hotels—and who also happens to be my very best friend!'

The moment Marly had dreaded had arrived, and head
high she turned to face him. The greeting she had re-
hearsed died on her lips. This man wasn't Alex! It was
a total stranger.

Unaware of her astonishment, he caught her hand in
a warm clasp. 'I'm delighted to meet you, though it beats
me why Andrea kept it secret that she knew you.
Incidentally, she wasn't exaggerating over the software
you created for us. It's reaping praise from staff and
guests alike in all our hotels.'

Still speechless, Marly went on staring at him. His
colouring was the same as the Alex she knew, but his
features were less definite and he was not as tall or as
well built.

'You must know my cousin,' he went on.

'Your c-cousin?'

'Alex. He was at our Bangkok hotel when you were
there. Not very clever, our mothers giving us the same
name.' He chuckled reminiscently. 'Particularly as he was
the serious type with little time for girls, and I was only
interested in sport and had an eye for the ladies when I
was in my pram! When we were at school together he

was always getting it in the neck for *my* misdeeds. It created quite a problem.'

Little did he know it was still creating problems! Marly thought miserably. For it had caused her to reject the proposal of the man she loved.

'Luckily in the business I'm called Alexander, and I'm doing my best to make Andrea call me that too.'

'I'm trying,' his wife protested, 'but you first introduced yourself as Alex, and it's stuck in my mind.'

'Not to worry. By our silver wedding you should get used to it!'

Andrea laughed and turned to Marly, suddenly noticing how pale she was. 'Are you feeling all right?'

'I'm fine. But I've had a long day and it's catching up with me.'

'Me too,' Alexander said. 'Let's go to dinner. A good meal will give us a lift.'

Marly would have liked nothing better than to say goodnight and go in search of Alex. Remembering the mocking things she had said when he had flown from Hawaii to see her in Bangkok—that she hadn't loved him and it had all been a pretence—she had to know why he had come to see her again last night. She had assumed it was because he wanted an adulterous affair with her, but now that she knew he wasn't married...

She knew more, of course: that he hadn't two-timed Andrea, that he wasn't a philanderer, and had meant all he had said to her in Phuket. Her heart pounded heavily and she drew a steadying breath. Had he come to see her last night because he still loved her despite believing she didn't care for him? If so, no wonder he had walked away when she had let him think Tony was her lover! Worse, that he had been her lover all the while she had been play-acting in Thailand!

Hardly aware of what she was doing, Marly found herself seated at a window-table in the Summit

Restaurant, and not until Andrea had twice asked her if she was happy to stick with champagne or preferred claret with her duck did she make an effort to return to the present, but oh, how hard it was when her every thought was with Alex, and how hurt he must have been when he had left her last night.

Suddenly she knew she could no longer sit here making meaningless conversation. She had to go to him at once.

'Your cousin came to see me last night,' she stated baldly. 'But I don't know where he's staying and I need to talk to him.'

Andrea flung her a puzzled glance and Marly met it with a bland one. Time to tell her friend the whole story later, when all the misunderstandings had been cleared away.

'You won't get him tonight, I'm afraid,' Alexander said, glancing at his watch. 'He's halfway to San Francisco by now.'

'San Francisco?'

'He's on a month's tour of our American hotels.'

Marly's spirits plunged. Had Alex been staying in one place she would have asked for a week off and flown to see him, but as it was, it seemed advisable to wait till he returned to England.

A thought struck her and she voiced it. 'Is he still based in Bangkok?'

'No. My uncle unexpectedly decided to retire and Alex took over the reins, which means he'll be here most of the time.' Grey eyes, very like his cousin's, probed her face. 'If you need to talk to him urgently, I can give you a number where you can contact him tomorrow.'

Aware that what she had to say could not be broached on the telephone, Marly shook her head. 'No, thanks, I'll wait till I see him.'

'He'll be back the day of our wedding reception—four weeks from Friday,' Andrea added. 'So you'll see him there.'

It was all Marly could think of as she drove home later, her thoughts with the man who was winging his way forty thousand feet above the Atlantic Ocean. Four weeks seemed light-years away. Perhaps she deserved the punishment of waiting. She had been so busy despising Alex for what she had imagined him to be that she had not seen him for the man he really was; a man who, once he gave his love to a woman, would love her enough to return to her even when she had thrown his love back in his face.

She tried to envisage their next meeting, wondering what she would do, what she would say. An image of his face as she had seen it last night, etched with lines, pain-shadowed, swamped her, and she knew that words alone could not atone for her actions. Yet words were all she had, and she prayed with every fibre of her being that the three words she would say to him would be sufficient to gain his forgiveness.

I love you.
I love you.
Please forgive me.

CHAPTER SIXTEEN

MARLY surveyed herself in the mirror. Her bed was strewn with dresses she had tried on and discarded, and finally she was satisfied. Not only was the cherry-red crêpe eye-catching enough to turn male heads, but the scooped neckline emphasised the full curves of her breasts—that owed nothing to a bra—and the clinging short skirt showed a disturbing expanse of shapely legs.

Her hair had presented a more intransigent problem. First she had allowed it to hang in a long, straight black silk curtain down her back. Secondly she had pulled it away from her face and twined it into a thick plait, but both styles had reminded her of an image Amalia Bradshaw was determined to put behind her.

Hot tongs had done the trick and now her hair was a riot of soft curls. Happily she ran her fingers through them. The bouncy feminine style emphasised her slenderness, and she applied her make-up to suit this picture, retaining her natural pallor but drawing attention to her full mouth and long, straight, doll-like eyelashes.

Promptly to time she entered the Park Suite on the tenth floor of the hotel. Her heart was racing, her limbs trembling, and every nerve-end frantically vibrating to pick up Alex Hamilton's presence. But in vain. There was neither sight nor sound of him.

Dismay robbed her of the joy that had filled her all day, though she masked it with her usual bright smile as she moved forward to congratulate the happy couple. Even in the midst of her turmoil she was quick to notice how happy Andrea and her husband were, and she hugged her friend close.

'Alex isn't here yet,' Andrea murmured, her comment signifying that she knew Marly's anxiety to see him had more to do with personal reasons than business ones. 'But he flew in last night so he'll definitely be coming. Still won't tell me what gives between the two of you?'

Since Andrea had repeated this question whenever they had talked on the telephone, Marly smiled and shook her head. 'For the tenth time, no. Now quit nagging and greet the rest of your guests.'

'There are several eligible Hamilton cousins I want to introduce to you.'

'Later. I'm not running away. I'll go say hello to your family and—good grief, is that Porky?' Marly stared at a bone-thin girl with a mass of curly brown hair who had been at school with them.

'She hasn't put on an ounce, has she?' Andrea chuckled. 'And she's the mother of triplets, can you believe?'

Marly hurried over to greet her and exchange news, then slowly did the same with Andrea's immediate family, all the while keeping her eye on the entrance to the suite.

An hour later there was still no sign of Alex, and she was sitting in a corner with a glass of champagne in her hand and one of the eligible Hamilton cousins—who had homed in on her without having to be introduced—when she turned her head and saw the object of her desire enter the room with a stunning redhead clinging to his arm.

'Will you?' her companion queried.

'Will I what? I'm sorry, my mind wandered.'

'*Very* flattering.'

'I'm sorry,' she repeated, unable to tear her eyes away from the tall, tawny-haired man in a silver-grey suit and the redhead in a dramatic black dress that made her skin glow like alabaster. 'What was the question again?'

'One that requires a yes. Will you have dinner with me?'

'I've another engagement.'

She didn't add that it would probably be with a tear-soaked pillow, for the affectionate way Alex was holding the girl's hand as they moved among the guests showed she was not a new acquaintance. Nor was she new to the elderly couple with whom they were now talking. Alex's parents obviously, for he bore a remarkable resemblance to the older man. His mother was kissing the redhead, who was smiling at her and then reaching up to lay a manicured hand on Alex's cheek.

In that instant Marly saw the marquise-shaped diamond on the girl's engagement finger, and felt as though her ribcage was being squeezed by giant pincers. She should have known Alex wouldn't bring a stranger to such a personal family gathering. But it wasn't in character for him to meet and become engaged to someone so quickly. Was she an old flame, perhaps? A relationship he had renewed when in the States? And why not, Marly thought miserably, when she herself had made it clear she didn't give a damn for him and had a lover anyway?

So much for her belief that his feelings for her were durable! Hadn't he said, when he had asked her to marry him, that he had proposed because it was the only way he could get her into his bed? Why hadn't she remembered *that*, for heaven's sake, instead of the other things he had said about wanting her, needing her? Anyway, it was plain as a pikestaff that in his terms wanting and needing simply meant lusting.

'You've spilled some of your drink,' her companion said. 'I'll fetch you another.'

The instant he was out of sight Marly decided to leave the reception. It was impossible for her to face Alex. Glancing around, she saw another exit leading into the corridor, and fleetly edged towards it, heaving a sigh of relief as she stepped outside. It was a short-lived relief however, for as she turned, Andrea rushed down the corridor and grabbed her arm.

'There you are! I've been looking everywhere for you. We'll soon be cutting the wedding cake and I'll be throwing my bouquet and want you standing close by.'

'Don't be so disgustingly romantic. The last thing I want is marriage.'

'Stop arguing.' Andrea pulled her sharply back into the room, knocking into Alex in the process. 'Nice to bump into you!' she quipped as he steadied her with his hands. 'No need to introduce you two. You know each other already.'

He nodded. 'Good to see you, Marly.' His voice was as cold as his expression.

'Same here.' Aware of Andrea watching them, Marly searched for something to say. 'How are Fiona and Kevin? Nan wrote and said they're engaged.'

'Yes. She's with Kevin in Australia, meeting his family.' Grey eyes slid over the flirty red dress and came to rest at a point beyond Marly's shoulder. 'I gather from my cousin that you're a friend of our lovely bride?'

'We were at boarding-school together.'

'I actually saw Marly in Bangkok when she was working for you,' Andrea intervened. 'Not that I knew you were there, of course. I'd only met one handsome Hamilton then, and was doing my best to forget him!' She gave Marly a comical look. 'Remember all the things I said about Alex when he ditched me? *My* Alex, I mean? I never thought I'd eventually marry him——!' She broke off. 'My beloved's signalling me like mad! I'd better see what he wants.'

She hurried away, leaving them alone, or as alone as two people could be among a crowd of three hundred! Marly didn't want to look at Alex, but she hungered for him so much that she could not stop her eyes feasting on him. If anything he was more gaunt than when he had come to see her, though it did not detract from his sex appeal. With his bone-structure he would be handsome as a corpse! It was a morbid thought, but how could she be anything else when a glittering diamond ring had rung the death-knell on her hope of happiness?

'May I fetch you a drink?' Alex was asking politely, seeing her empty hands.

'No, thanks. I'm leaving. I was on my way when Andrea collared me.'

'She'll be disappointed if you don't try to catch her bouquet—even though it's a disgustingly romantic tradition.'

So he had heard Andrea's comment and her response to it. Marly's cheeks burned, and she knew that if she didn't put distance between herself and this man she would start howling like a baby.

'I—I really have to leave.'

'Where's the boyfriend?'

'I'm seeing him later.' It was pointless telling him who Tony really was.

'I'm surprised Andrea didn't invite him.'

Ignoring this, Marly turned to go, but her exit was barred by Alex, his expression implacable.

'The things Andrea said about my cousin ditching her wouldn't have been the reason for that charade of yours, would it?'

'I don't know what you mean.'

'I'd believe you more easily if you didn't have red roses blooming in your cheeks!' He came a step closer, forcing her back upon the wall, his body blocking her from the rest of the room. 'Be honest with me, dammit. You mistook me for my cousin, didn't you? It won't be the first time I've been punished for his deeds, though it hasn't happened since we left school and he started calling himself Alexander.' Reading the answer on her face, Alex gave a gusty sigh and leaned against the wall as if he was too tired to stand upright. 'So it was that simple,' he muttered. 'You thought I'd played fast and loose with Andrea and determined to give me a taste of my own medicine.'

He fell silent again, and Marly, watching him from beneath her lashes, saw he was gradually working out all the reasons for her behaviour. As long as he didn't realise she had genuinely fallen in love with him, she could bear it, for that was something she never wanted him to know.

'When I was in London at the same time as my cousin, and he married Andrea, you thought it was me,' Alex continued, 'and likewise when we both went to Hawaii to deal with the mess there.' The clipped voice faltered. 'When I flew from Hawaii to see you, you saw me as the faithless bridegroom, didn't you?'

'Yes,' Marly confessed, and before she could say another word was propelled swiftly from the room and down the corridor. 'Where are you taking me?' she cried as he ignored the lift and pulled her up a flight of stairs.

'I'm staying in a suite on the next floor. We can talk better there.'

'There's no more for us to say.' Marly was desperate not to be alone with him. 'I'm truly sorry I mistook you for your cousin, but no real harm was done and——'

'Shut up!' he rasped, and unlocking a door, pushed her into a luxuriously furnished sitting-room.

Marly's instinct was to make a run for it, but fearing this might be a give-away of her feelings she nonchalantly moved across to the window and stared at the London skyline.

'You've already shown me what a great actress you are,' Alex said behind her, 'so I won't attempt to guess how you feel towards me. But I won't let you leave here until I've told you how I feel about *you*. You bowled me over the moment you walked on to the stage at that Christmas show, and with every subsequent meeting I fell more deeply in love with you.'

'You've no right to say that,' Marly cried.

'Because of your lover? Well, I'm sorry, but I can't play the chivalrous gentleman. I don't believe you were putting on an act when you lay in my arms that night on the boat, and I——'

'You really are an uncaring bastard, aren't you?'

'Because I love you too much to let you go without fighting for you?'

'It's more than that,' she flung at him. 'If you love me so much, how come you were so quick to get engaged?'

An indrawn breath was his only reply as he strode over to her and caught her shoulders in a painful grip. 'Do you enjoy acting judge and jury?' He shook her roughly with every word. 'I can understand it when you thought I'd played fast and loose with Andrea, but now that you know I didn't—that you were totally wrong about me—how come you're *still* judging me as if I have no moral scruples?' Flinging her aside, he turned away from her. 'Isobel, my so-called fiancée, happens to be my cousin,' he stated in a flat voice. 'She works in New York as a model and will shortly be marrying the doctor who took out her gallstones six months ago.'

Marly wished she could sink into the ground. Alex had a right to be angry with her and there was nothing she could say in mitigation of her behaviour. She just had to eat dirt!

'I'm an idiot, Alex. I suppose I've grown so used to thinking the worst of you that I can't think the best.' She moved closer to him and put a tentative hand on his back. He tensed at her touch but did not turn. 'You were pretty quick to judge *me* when you came to my apartment,' she went on. 'These days men and women often share accommodation but it doesn't mean anything. Tony and I and Jenny Hunter—she works at 3S too—bought the place jointly, though I'll probably sell them my share when they get married in three months' time.'

Alex swung round, his face alight. 'You mean you aren't lovers?'

Not waiting for her retort, his mouth found hers in a fierce kiss that demanded her surrender. Willingly she gave it, her body burrowing into his the better to feel his wild arousal, to breathe in the scent of his desire.

With a muffled groan he picked her up in his arms, strode with her into the bedroom and placed her on the quilted king-size bed.

Coming down beside her, he drew her close. 'I almost didn't come to the reception today,' he confessed against her lips. 'This past month I've alternated between loving you like crazy and hating you like mad.'

'That describes *my* emotions when I was with you in Thailand.'

'When did you discover you had mixed me up with my cousin?'

'Four weeks ago—the day you left for San Francisco. That was the first time I met Alexander. I nearly flew out to see you but he said you had a hectic schedule and——'

'I'd have made time for *you*, and it would have saved me a month of aggro.'

'It was heartbreaking for me too,' Marly whispered, tenderly touching her fingertips to the dark shadows beneath his eyes. 'Are you sure, Alex?'

Amazed, he pulled back, the better to see her face. 'I proposed to you when we were in Phuket, so why should I have changed my mind?'

'Because I . . .' She hesitated, then plunged on. 'When you asked me to be your wife, you admitted that marriage was the last thing you'd had in mind, but you couldn't see any other way of having me. Well, I want you to know that—that that's no longer true. I'm not Marly, the old-fashioned traditionalist, but Amalia Bradshaw, a modern woman who loves you enough to trust you and to live with you on your terms.'

'I see.' Alex stroked his hand over her silky black hair. 'What I said then was like the final gasp of a dying man! In my personal life I'd always been my own boss and never had to account to anyone else, and the idea of sharing my freedom with a woman scared the hell out of me, which was why I made that stupid remark. But when you said you wanted to think it over and I faced the thought of being rejected, I realised that life without you would be a prison of loneliness, whereas life with you would enable me to enjoy every hour of every day.'

A poet could not have put it more lyrically, yet there was one more thing she had to ascertain. 'Is it me you love or the girl I was pretending to be? I'm definitely not the submissive type, you know.'

'Thank goodness for that! Your agreeableness was the one thing that flummoxed me, for I often felt you were biting your tongue rather than saying what you really meant.' He tilted up her chin and scanned her face. 'Do I have to say anything else to convince you of my love?'

Marly placed her palms together and lowered her head to them in the last *wai* she would ever make to him.

'Sometimes actions speak louder than words, Mr Hamilton.'

In silence he found the zip at the back of her dress and slowly undid it. Soon she was lying naked beside him, and he caressed her firm breasts with their pink pointed nipples, her rounded stomach and her curved hips, scantily covered by black lace. Smoky grey irises darkened as he placed his mouth to the soft mound of dark hair at the junction of her legs, murmuring deep in his throat as he felt the tremor that went through her.

Filled with love, Marly began undoing the buttons of his jacket. She slipped it off his shoulders and then removed his shirt, the silk fabric no smoother than his skin. She had never undressed anyone, and as her fingers fumbled at the narrow leather belt around his waist she could not stop the warm tide of colour that rushed into her cheeks.

Aware of her embarrassment, he did it for her, though as his nude body covered hers desire for him became paramount and all she could think of was becoming a part of him. Sensuously she rubbed her breasts across his chest, her nipples hardening as she felt the surge of his arousal. Her fingers moved to it, and as she touched him he brought his mouth down on hers, his tongue hot and demanding, becoming ferociously aggressive as passion gathered strength.

Alex was a superb lover, teasing, tantalising, caressing with mouth, teeth and tongue until they were both inflamed to fever-pitch and only the ultimate surrender would satisfy.

Parting her legs, she wound them round his thighs as he lay between hers. Instantly the rock-hard length of his manhood plunged into her and she gasped and cried out, moaning with joy as he thrust in and out in everdecreasing movements until he was pounding at the very heart of her, touching the innermost core with a rod of fire that vibrated into a single screaming crescendo of fulfilment that exploded into a rapturous, shuddering climax.

In the aftermath of intimacy, they lay supine in each other's arms. 'I wish I'd flown to the States to see you,' Marly said soberly. 'I can't forget those awful four weeks.'

'Me neither,' he agreed, kissing the top of her head. 'But it was worth the wait.'

'I seem to remember you telling me that waiting simply made it quicker!' she teased.

'*Was* I too quick for you?' he asked instantly.

'I can't remember. Perhaps if you jogged my memory...'

They dissolved into laughter, and as it ceased, Marly glanced at her wristwatch and gave a little cry. 'Oh, Alex, we've missed Andrea cutting the cake and throwing her bouquet!'

'Never mind,' he consoled, rolling off the bed and taking her with him. 'Let's get dressed and go and tell her you'll soon be throwing your own!'

MILLS & BOON

EXCITING NEW COVERS

To reflect the ever-changing contemporary romance series we've designed new covers which perfectly capture the warmth, glamour and sophistication of modern-day romantic situations.

We know, because we've designed them with your comments in mind, that you'll just love the bright, warm, romantic colours and the up-to-date new look.

WATCH OUT FOR THESE NEW COVERS

From October 1993   Price £1.80

Available from W.H. Smith, John Menzies, Martins, Forbuoys,
most supermarkets and other paperback stockists.
Also available from Mills & Boon Reader Service, Freepost, PO Box 236,
Thornton Road, Croydon, Surrey CR9 9EL. (UK Postage & Packing free)

THREE SENSUOUS STORIES...

ONE BEAUTIFUL VOLUME

A special collection of three individual love stories, beautifully presented in one absorbing volume.

One of the world's most popular romance authors, Charlotte Lamb has written over 90 novels, including the bestselling *Barbary Wharf* six part mini-series. This unique edition features three of her earlier titles, together for the first time in one collectable volume.

AVAILABLE FROM SEPTEMBER 1993   PRICED £4.99

W❍RLDWIDE

*Available from W. H. Smith, John Menzies, Martins, Forbuoys,
most supermarkets and other paperback stockists.
Also available from Worldwide Reader Service, FREEPOST, PO Box 236,
Thornton Road, Croydon, Surrey CR9 9EL. (UK Postage & Packing free)*

4 FREE

Romances and 2 FREE gifts just for you!

You can enjoy all the heartwarming emotion of true love for FREE! Discover the heartbreak and happiness, the emotion and the tenderness of the modern relationships in Mills & Boon Romances.

We'll send you 4 Romances as a special offer from Mills & Boon Reader Service, along with the opportunity to have 6 captivating new Romances delivered to your door each month.

Claim your FREE books and gifts overleaf...

An irresistible offer from Mills & Boon

Become a regular reader of Romances with Mills & Boon Reader Service and we'll welcome you with 4 books, a CUDDLY TEDDY and a special MYSTERY GIFT all absolutely FREE.

And then look forward to receiving 6 brand new Romances each month, delivered to your door hot off the presses, postage and packing FREE! Plus our free Newsletter featuring author news, competitions, special offers and much more.

This invitation comes with no strings attached. You may cancel or suspend your subscription at any time, and still keep your free books and gifts.

It's so easy. Send no money now. Simply fill in the coupon below and post it to -
Reader Service, FREEPOST, PO Box 236, Croydon, Surrey CR9 9EL.

NO STAMP REQUIRED

Free Books Coupon

Yes! Please rush me 4 FREE Romances and 2 FREE gifts! Please also reserve me a Reader Service subscription. If I decide to subscribe I can look forward to receiving 6 brand new Romances for just £10.80 each month, postage and packing FREE. If I decide not to subscribe I shall write to you within 10 days - I can keep the free books and gifts whatever I choose. I may cancel or suspend my subscription at any time. I am over 18 years of age.

Ms/Mrs/Miss/Mr _____ EP56R

Address _____

_____

Postcode _____ Signature _____

Offers closes 31st March 1994. The right is reserved to refuse an application and change the terms of this offer. This offer does not apply to Romance subscribers. One application per household. Overseas readers please write for details. Southern Africa write to Book Services International Ltd., Box 41654, Craighall, Transvaal 2024. You may be mailed with offers from other reputable companies as a result of this application. Please tick box if you would prefer not to receive such offers. ☐

Another Face . . .
Another Identity . . .
Another Chance . . .

When her teenage love turns to hate, Geraldine Frances vows to even the score. After arranging her own "death", she embarks on a dramatic transformation emerging as *Silver*, a hauntingly beautiful and mysterious woman few men would be able to resist.

With a new face and a new identity, she is now ready to destroy the man responsible for her tragic past.

Silver – a life ruled by one all-consuming passion, is Penny Jordan at her very best.

WORLDWIDE

Available from W. H. Smith, John Menzies, Martins, Forbuoys, most supermarkets and other paperback stockists.
Also available from Worldwide Reader Service, FREEPOST, PO Box 236, Thornton Road, Croydon, Surrey CR9 9EL. (UK Postage & Packing free)

£3.99

Next Month's Romances

Each month you can choose from a wide variety of romance with Mills & Boon. Below are the new titles to look out for next month, why not ask either Mills & Boon Reader Service or your Newsagent to reserve you a copy of the titles you want to buy – just tick the titles you would like and either post to Reader Service or take it to any Newsagent and ask them to order your books.

Please save me the following titles:	Please tick	√
A DIFFICULT MAN	Lindsay Armstrong	
MARRIAGE IN JEOPARDY	Miranda Lee	
TENDER ASSAULT	Anne Mather	
RETURN ENGAGEMENT	Carole Mortimer	
LEGACY OF SHAME	Diana Hamilton	
A PART OF HEAVEN	Jessica Marchant	
CALYPSO'S ISLAND	Rosalie Ash	
CATCH ME IF YOU CAN	Anne McAllister	
NO NEED FOR LOVE	Sandra Marton	
THE FABERGE CAT	Anne Weale	
AND THE BRIDE WORE BLACK	Helen Brooks	
LOVE IS THE ANSWER	Jennifer Taylor	
BITTER POSSESSION	Jenny Cartwright	
INSTANT FIRE	Liz Fielding	
THE BABY CONTRACT	Suzanne Carey	
NO TRESPASSING	Shannon Waverly	

If you would like to order these books in addition to your regular subscription from Mills & Boon Reader Service please send £1.80 per title to: Mills & Boon Reader Service, Freepost, P.O. Box 236, Croydon, Surrey, CR9 9EL, quote your Subscriber No:................................... (If applicable) and complete the name and address details below. Alternatively, these books are available from many local Newsagents including W.H.Smith, J.Menzies, Martins and other paperback stockists from 8 October 1993.

Name:..

Address:..

....Post Code:........................

To Retailer: If you would like to stock M&B books please contact your regular book/magazine wholesaler for details.

You may be mailed with offers from other reputable companies as a result of this application. If you would rather not take advantage of these opportunities please tick box ☐